Club

Whale Song

Other books in
The Flip-Flop Club series:

Charmed Summer

Coming soon . . .

Midnight Messages
Star Struck

Ellen Richardson

Series created by Working Partners Ltd

OXFORD
UNIVERSITY PRESS

OXFORD
UNIVERSITY PRESS

Great Clarendon Street, Oxford OX2 6DP
Oxford University Press is a department of the University of Oxford.
It furthers the University's objective of excellence in research, scholarship,
and education by publishing worldwide in

Oxford   New York

Auckland   Cape Town   Dar es Salaam   Hong Kong   Karachi
Kuala Lumpur   Madrid   Melbourne   Mexico City   Nairobi
New Delhi   Shanghai   Taipei   Toronto

With offices in

Argentina   Austria   Brazil   Chile   Czech Republic   France   Greece
Guatemala   Hungary   Italy   Japan   Poland   Portugal   Singapore
South Korea   Switzerland   Thailand   Turkey   Ukraine   Vietnam

Oxford is a registered trade mark of Oxford University Press
in the UK and in certain other countries

British Library Cataloguing in Publication Data
Data available

ISBN: 978-0-19-275662-6
1 3 5 7 9 10 8 6 4 2

Printed in Great Britain

Paper used in the production of this book is a natural,
recyclable product made from wood grown in sustainable forests.
The manufacturing process conforms to the environmental
regulations of the country of origin.

For my niece,
Catherine

Chapter 1

'It's not worth being famous if I have to get up at five a.m.,' Sierra grumbled, yawning and shivering in the chilly dawn air. 'And I'm not even sure I want my picture in the paper looking like this!' She tugged at her too-short, Tash-sized wetsuit, staring mournfully at her feet which were very un-Sierra-like in neoprene wetshoes instead of sparkly flip-flops.

Elly smiled in sympathy but grabbed her friend's hand and pulled her after Tash. 'Come on! She's leaving us behind!'

'You have to get up early to go whale-

spotting.' Tash strode ahead of them across the beach. 'I hope the rumours are true and that there really are Northern Bottlenose whales headed our way. They're rare this far south.'

'We just *have* to win *The Sunday Island News* contest and be the first to get a photograph of them,' Elly said.

'I'll do my best!' Tash patted the waterproof camera she wore around her neck.

'It's the photo of *us* I'm worried about!' Sierra muttered.

'Don't worry,' Tash said, whirling round to grin at Sierra. 'The news crew will have a hair stylist and someone to do manicures.'

'Really?' Sierra's face lit up, then fell. 'Oh, I nearly fell for that. OK. We find the whales first, then I stress. Deal?'

'Deal!' Elly was suddenly so excited she felt she might explode. She let go of

Sierra and leapt over a mound of seaweed, whooping in delight. The wetsuit Tash had lent her made her feel like a real sailor. And today they were going to leave the harbour for open sea. Her tummy went all butterflies and squirms at the thought.

The morning sun hung just above the eastern sea and the beach of Sunday Island's main harbour was washed clean by the tide. Sailing boat rigging clinked in the steady off-shore breeze and seagulls screamed overhead. Other than a small fleet of dinghies dozing on the sand and a flock of wading birds dodging the waves, the girls were alone. Mojo, Tash's border terrier, spotted the birds and gave chase, bounding across the damp sand. With a clattering of wings, the birds took to the air before wheeling off to find a dog-free stretch of sand.

Elly slid to a stop, watching the birds.

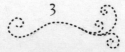

Everything smelt of sea and freshness. What a morning for an adventure!

'I've seen Minke whales before, but never a Northern Bottlenose. It would be so great if we spotted one.' Tash's voice was wistful. Elly knew that Tash had photographs of whales and dolphins stuck all over the walls of her bedroom and tree house. Today was obviously pretty special for her.

Tash whistled Mojo to heel as they reached her blue and white Wayfarer dinghy, named the *Mojo* after him. He trotted over to them, panting and wagging his tail. 'Good dog!' Tash gave him a pat, then slid off her backpack and stowed it in the boat. 'OK, give me your stuff too.' She turned around and her eyes widened in disbelief at the sight of Sierra's enormous purple handbag, which her friend was wearing slung over her wetsuit.

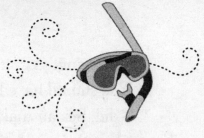

'Why on earth did you bring *that*?' Tash began to splutter with laughter.

'I've got lots of really important stuff in here,' Sierra said, hugging her handbag close. 'I need to keep it with me.'

Elly shrugged her backpack off her shoulders. In her rush to make the dawn rendezvous she hadn't bothered to fasten it properly. Now, as she struggled to close the zip, the backpack slipped from her fingers. It hit the ground, dumping all her stuff onto the sand.

'Watch out, you'll get sand in our sandwiches!' Sierra knelt to help Elly repack. She held up a book. 'What's this?'

'A book?' Tash exclaimed. 'The *Mojo* isn't exactly a cruise liner, you know. No deckchairs and skittles.'

'No fancy restaurant with five-course meals either.' Sierra sighed, rubbing her tummy.

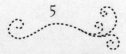

'I'm starving!'

'You should have had breakfast,' Tash said.

'I did! Sea air makes me hungry.'

'Everything makes you hungry.' Elly shook her head in mock despair. 'You're going to have to become a chef.'

'Great idea.' Sierra's eyes sparkled. 'With my own TV show.' She waved to an invisible camera, and then handed the book to Elly.

'I brought the book to show you both,' Elly said. 'Aunt Dina gave it to me last night. It's an Edith Builtmore sailing adventure. My aunt says Edith Builtmore used to live on Sunday Island.'

'Which one is it?' Tash reached for the book. '*The Secret of Harebell Island*. That's one of my favourites. I have every book Edith Builtmore ever wrote. She was into marine ecology long before

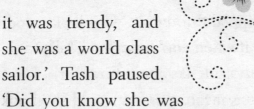

it was trendy, and she was a world class sailor.' Tash paused. 'Did you know she was returning to Sunday Island after sailing the Atlantic single-handed when she disappeared? They never found any trace of her or her yacht.'

'That's sad.' Sierra shivered. 'And mysterious. I wonder what happened to her? Maybe she's still stranded on a desert island somewhere.'

'She'd be super-old by now,' Elly said. She tried to imagine being out in the open sea all alone. Edith Builtmore must have been very brave.

Tash turned the book over and studied the author's photograph. 'Someday I'm going to sail around the world single-handed.'

'Now I know you're crazy.' Sierra made a face. 'Days without anyone to talk to? Or a hot shower? Urgh!' She took the book from

Tash and flipped through it. 'This looks good. Can I read it when you're finished, Elly?'

'Sure,' Elly said. 'It's about three girls. I just wondered...is it too weird or could she have been writing about our mums? They would have been on the island about the same time she was. It would be so cool if they inspired one of Edith Builtmore's books.'

Elly thought about the photograph the three of them had found in Tash's attic, the one of their mothers as girls on Sunday Island. They had been best friends too. She had framed a copy of the photo and hung it on the wall of her bedroom in Aunt Dina's cottage. It was her second most precious possession.

She reached up to touch the chain of the silver charm she always wore around her neck. She'd tucked it inside her wetsuit to keep it safe. Each of them had inherited

a friendship charm
from their mothers,
and had sworn never to
take them off. Tash's charm was
pinned to her wetsuit and Sierra's dangled
among the clutter of bangles on her wrist.

Sierra's eyes were bright with excitement. 'I bet you're right. Our mums are secretly famous.'

'And if we want to be famous too, we need to get going before someone else beats us to those whales!' Tash interrupted. 'We need to be the first to spot them, remember?'

Elly slid the book into her backpack. She fastened the zip securely before handing the pack to Tash, who stored it in one of the waterproof cargo bags tucked against the side of the boat.

Then Tash tugged out some life jackets and handed them round. 'Essential equipment, guys.'

'But this thing is...*orange!*' Sierra's eyes

9

widened in horror. 'Orange makes my skin look green.'

'Sorry, Sierra.' Tash was doing her best not to smile. 'Even Mojo has to wear one.' She knelt to slip a bright orange dog-shaped life jacket onto the border terrier's back, fastening it with chest and belly straps. Mojo whined but stood patiently, obviously used to the routine. 'Safety before fashion.'

'I guess,' Sierra said sadly as she pulled on the life jacket. 'Oh well, at least my armbands are pink.'

'Armbands?' Elly said, before she could stop herself. Tash was staring, open-mouthed.

'Absolutely,' Sierra said firmly. 'Essential for the ocean-going lady of fashion.' She tugged some bits of plastic from a mesh pocket on her wetsuit and proceeded to blow up a pair of neon-pink armbands, which she slid up her arms. When she had finished, she struck a muscle-pose. 'What d'ya think?'

Elly began to splutter. Tash was already whooping in hysterics.

Sierra grinned at them. 'OK, so I'm a scaredy-cat, but the armbands make me happier about going out to sea in this teensy little boat.'

'Totally you, Sierra.' Elly decided this wasn't the time to mention that neon-pink armbands and a fluorescent orange vest were an eye-watering combination.

'Come on,' said Tash, when she got her breath back. 'Let's get the *Mojo* launched before the rest of the island wakes up and beats us to the whales.'

Mojo lifted his ears at the sound of his name and barked.

'All dogs on board!' Tash scooped the border

terrier into the bottom of the boat, where he sat perfectly still, like the trained sailor he was. Tash lifted the front bar of the two-wheeled trailer and began to back her boat towards the sea. As soon as she was knee-deep in the water, Tash unhooked the ties and floated the boat off the trailer. She steadied the dinghy in the bobbing waves as Elly and Sierra towed the trailer back up onto the beach. Then they splashed into the sea and held the boat while Tash hopped in. She stood in the centre of the boat, untying the ropes securing the sail. She took her place at the tiller. 'Come aboard and raise the mainsail, First Officer Elly!'

Sierra kept the dinghy steady as Elly hitched herself over the side of the boat and found the rope used to raise and lower the dinghy's large triangular sail. She pulled it in hand over hand, as Tash had taught her. The mainsail slowly unfurled and began to flap in the breeze. When it reached the top of the mast, Elly secured the rope and settled back, her heart thudding with excitement as the sail filled and the boat started to slide through the water.

Sierra quickly hauled herself over the side. 'You can't leave without me!'

'Raise the jib, Second Officer Sierra!' Tash called.

Sierra made quick work of raising the tiny jib sail, which was soon ballooning out in front of the mast. The dinghy picked up speed, riding as gently as a rocking horse over the bouncing waves. The *Mojo* steered crisply away from shore.

Elly sat back on the wooden ledge that served as a seat. Sierra sat opposite her, clutching the sides of the boat with both hands. Tash guided them towards choppier water at the

head of the harbour. The boat cut through the waves, bobbing up and down, as the *Mojo* headed out into open sea. The whale-sighting expedition had begun!

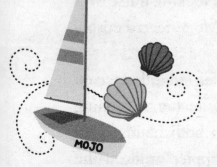

MOJO

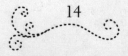

Chapter 2

The wind picked up as they left the shelter of the harbour. Elly's tummy lurched as the boat swooped to the top of a big wave and slid down the other side. It was like being on a roller coaster. Captain Tash had a happy grin on her face. Mojo zigzagged across from one side of the boat to the other, tail perked with delight, begging first Elly, then Sierra, for an ear-rub. Sierra kept one hand fastened to the side of the boat as she bent down to pet Mojo. She looked a bit green—was she feeling seasick or was it the orange life jacket?

Elly relaxed, enjoying the feel of the wind

in her face as it whipped her hair back. There was so much to see and it was all beautiful: the sea all around them swirled with rich greens and blues. The *Mojo* was curving westward now, heading away from the mainland towards a cluster of uninhabited islands in the distance: windswept humps rising out of the water. They look like the backs of enormous sea monsters, Elly thought.

'That's where we're heading,' said Tash, noticing where she was looking. 'That group of three islands.'

'What are they called?' Sierra fished out a pair of enormous designer sunglasses with purple lenses from her handbag. She slipped them onto her nose and peered at the islands.

'They're called the Western Isles,' Tash shouted over the slapping sound of

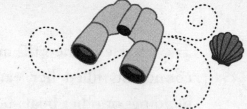

the *Mojo's* bow slicing through the waves.

Elly noticed a long string of rocks spearing out of the sea halfway between them and the Western Isles. Waves broke against the rocks, shooting white spray into the air. Long before they got near the treacherous looking rocks, Tash turned the tiller and the *Mojo* angled right, sailing clear of the danger.

'That line of rocks is called the Devil's Teeth,' Tash called. 'They wrecked loads of ships in the old days. And they're still dangerous in fog or storms. You often see seals sunning on them. The tourist boats come out to watch them.'

Elly spotted several flocks of cormorants standing on the jagged rocks, spreading their wings and raising their heads to the sun. They look like prehistoric birds, Elly thought. Or flying dinosaurs.

The sun beat down. The wind gusted.

The crackle of the sails and the cries of the cormorants filled her ears. There were no buildings or other boats in sight. They could have sailed back in time thousands of years. The thought sent a delightful chill down her spine.

'Devil's Teeth!' cried Sierra. 'Lovely and scary! But why name a pile of rocks and not the islands they're guarding? "Western Isles" is boring. I vote we name them after us. Three islands—three of us. Since it's my idea, I get first pick.'

As the dinghy sailed past the last of the rocks, Sierra pointed to the nearest island. 'I like that one. It has a tiny sandy beach. If it had a palm tree it would look just like the perfect paradise island.'

'We hereby name you Sierra Island! Hooray!' Elly cheered and waved at the island.

'And the big island
next to it should be
called Tash Island.'

'Why?' Tash gave a
mock scowl. 'Are you calling me fat?'

'No, because with that huge triangular
shaped rock growing right out of the middle,
the whole island looks like a sailing boat.'

'Hey.' Tash's eyes widened in amazement.
'I've never noticed that before. You're right—
it should be called Sailing Boat Island.'

'No,' said Sierra. 'Tash Island. Three girls,
three islands, remember?'

Tash shrugged. But she was grinning with
delight.

'So the far one is Elly Island. A distant isle
shrouded in mystery.' Sierra cocked her head.
'You happy with that, Elly?'

Elly laughed. 'Sure. Why not?'

'We'll be going to Elly Island later,' Tash
said. 'But we're heading for Tash Island first.
We're going to anchor in a little cove on the

19

north side of the island and climb the rock. You get the best views over the western seas from up there. If those whales are still in the area, we should be able to find them. The best bet is that they'll stay on this side of Sunday Island because it's closer to the Atlantic.' She shook her head, and her voice grew wistful. 'I really want to see these whales. Northern Bottlenose whales are gorgeous, like giant dolphins.'

'You may have the fancy camera, Tash, but I bet I'm the one who gets the perfect shot.' Sierra flashed her mobile phone at them.

'You're on, Sierra,' Tash said. 'I'll bet you a double order of chips that I get the best photo. So let's get spotting! There are binoculars in the cargo bag under where you're sitting,' Tash said to Elly.

'What am I looking

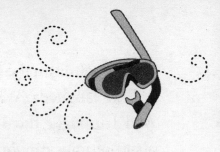

for?' Elly asked, as she pulled out the binoculars and strung them round her neck.

'Whales breathe air,' Tash explained. 'They're mammals, not fish.'

Elly watched her friend's eyes light up as she talked.

'They hold their breath for ages during a dive then when they surface for air they shoot up a small spout of water out of a blow-hole on their backs. Sort of like a fountain.' Tash's free hand made a graceful arc in the air. 'Look for that, or just their backs as they jump out of the waves. Hey, Sierra,' Tash continued, 'underneath where you're sitting is some snorkelling gear. A mouthpiece and mask each.'

'Snorkelling?' Sierra rooted in the canvas cargo bag. She pulled out three masks with snorkels attached and held them out in front of her as if they stank. 'This is unacceptable!

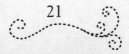

I'm not getting in the water with those whales.'

Tash laughed. 'Whales don't eat people. And I brought the snorkels because there's a sort of mini canyon in the sea floor in the shallow water off Elly Island. If we have time after we find the whales, I'd like to do some exploring.'

'I'd rather find treasure buried on my island,' Sierra said. 'A treasure chest full of gold doubloons. Then we could be famous *and* rich!' She tucked the snorkelling gear into her handbag.

Elly grinned. That handbag was bottomless. She began to scan the waves using the binoculars. They were just drawing near Sierra Island. The wind had picked up and was beginning to gust, making the triangular mainsail snap with a noise like a rifle shot. The dinghy flew

MOJO

through the water, bouncing over the top of the waves. After five minutes of this, Sierra gave a seasick sort of groan, but Elly was too busy looking for any glimpse of a whale to take much notice.

'Lower the jib sail, Sierra,' Tash ordered. Something in her voice made Elly lower the binoculars and stare at their captain. Tash was frowning at the darkening sky. 'I hope it doesn't rain,' she said. 'The forecast was good this morning.'

Elly looked to see if Sierra needed a hand, but her friend was already busy with the ropes.

The *Mojo* slowed with only the mainsail raised and Elly concentrated on scanning the water. She kept thinking she saw a whale beneath the waves, but it was only floating patches of seaweed or shadows from the clouds rapidly gathering overhead. And then: 'A spout! That was a spout!' She'd seen it

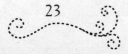

clearly: a white fountain of water shooting into the air.

'Where? Let me see!' Sierra leapt across the bottom of the dinghy and knelt next to Elly. She leant over the side, mobile phone at the ready.

'Sierra!' shouted Tash. 'Sit down!' But it was too late. A huge wave reared out of the sea. The dinghy lurched sideways, and Sierra screamed as she began to topple into the water.

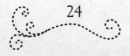

Chapter 3

Elly grabbed Sierra's life jacket. Her friend hung overboard from the waist up, flailing her arms in an attempt to grab hold of the side of the boat and screaming in terror. The *Mojo* continued to tilt towards the sea like a saucepan tipping out its contents. Elly wanted to scream too, but she was too busy holding on to her friend. Her arms were shaking with the effort. She felt herself begin to slide after Sierra. Just when she thought they would both tumble head-first into the sea, the *Mojo* reached the bottom of the wave and, with a groan and a lurch, began the dizzy business

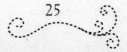

of righting itself. Once the dinghy was more or less upright, Elly found it easy to tug Sierra back aboard.

Sierra collapsed onto the bottom of the dinghy, shuddering and sobbing. 'I dropped my phone!' she cried. 'It's in the sea.'

'Better it than you,' Tash said. Her face and voice were grim. 'You forgot everything I taught you in the harbour, Sierra. You can't jump around like that, especially in bad weather. And we've got some coming now. Look!' She pointed west. 'One of Sunday Island's freak storms is heading right for us.'

An enormous dark cloud had boiled up and was rushing towards them impossibly fast. It's like something out of Mum's movies, Elly thought. But for real! She froze, staring at the storm roaring towards them, feeling small, scared, and

very exposed in the
tiny dinghy. The sun
had disappeared and
the wind was cracking
Mojo's sail like thunder.

'Elly!' Tash shouted over the increasing
roar of the wind. 'Get the mainsail down to
quarter mast. Quick!'

Elly unwound the rope from its cleat
with fingers clumsy with fear. The wind was
tearing at the dinghy's sail, sending the boat
flying across the water. The sky had grown
twilight dark and it felt as if night had fallen.
Cold rain lashed down, stinging her face
and hands. The waves were swelling, rolling,
towering higher and higher in the sky. Elly
couldn't remember ever being this scared.
She slackened off the mainsail, then tried to
lower it, but the wind fought her.

Sierra had taken her old place on the
opposite side of the boat. 'Sierra!' Elly cried
over the howling wind. 'I need a hand with

27

this.' Sierra nodded, a look of determination replacing the fear on her face as she crouched down and edged over to Elly. Sierra grabbed the rope and together they tugged until the sail began to lower into neat folds above the boom. With Sierra's help, it only took a few minutes to lower the mainsail to quarter mast and secure it.

The wind was pushing the dinghy over. Its left side slanted out of the water at a steep angle. Elly clambered upwards, struggling to reach Sierra and Tash, who were perched on the starboard gunwale. All three of them sat on the edge of the boat and leant back over the surging waves, trying to keep the dinghy from being blown right over.

Elly held on with frozen fingers. She didn't dare look down at the waves churning a few feet beneath her.

'Well done, crew!' Tash

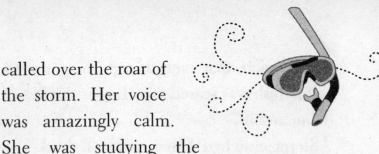

called over the roar of the storm. Her voice was amazingly calm. She was studying the incoming waves and holding tight to the tiller with her right hand. Mojo crouched in the bottom of the boat, his shoulders hunched against the rain, his big brown eyes fixed anxiously on Tash.

The rain poured down harder than ever, driven into Elly's back on gusts of wind. It felt like being drenched by a giant garden hose. She glanced sideways at Sierra. The wind had grabbed her friend's long hair and it streamed in front of her face like a tattered flag. Sierra was hunched over, her arms wrapped protectively around her handbag.

Tash leant forwards in the sheeting rain. 'I can't tell which way we are going,' she yelled. 'The Western Isles are death-traps for boats in this sort of storm.' Her face was white and intent and Elly saw, with a lurch of

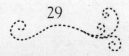

her stomach, that even though she sounded calm, Tash was scared too. 'Lower the last of the mainsail!'

Sierra clutched Elly's hand. 'I think I'm going to be seasick,' she groaned. Her face really was green now. Elly felt queasy herself. The little dinghy rode up towering waves and slipped into the troughs at a sickening speed.

'I'll do it!' Elly said. Sierra nodded in gratitude.

Elly scooted across the bottom of the dinghy and lowered the mainsail completely. Even without a sail, the storm continued to chase the *Mojo* over the waves. The dinghy swirled  through the water, lurching up and down and sideways at the same time. Elly stumbled and fell to her knees as she staggered back to Sierra. Pain shot through her right knee as it landed on something hard, but she was

too frightened to care.
She pushed herself up
again. Sierra grabbed
her hand and tugged
her into her seat. They
would have to try their luck with no sails. But
what if it didn't work? Would the *Mojo* be
able to ride out the storm?

A huge wave reared up out of nowhere. The
boat tilted onto its side, threatening to spill
all its contents. Elly screamed and grabbed
for the nearest rope. As she clung to it, she
tumbled into the sea, and felt the entire
dinghy judder as the mast smacked into the
water. They had capsized!

The waves closed over her head. She
kicked upwards, keeping hold of the rope,
and surfaced to find the storm raging as fierce
as ever. Rain poured onto her. It battered the
overturned dinghy, which was floating on the
waves like a broken bird.

Elly spat out seawater and clung to the

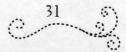

dinghy with frozen hands. It's the only thing keeping me from being swept out to sea, she thought. But how long can I hold on? The boat lurched up and down in the huge waves. The wind howled overhead. Where were Tash and Sierra? Her heart thudded harder and she bit back the urge to scream. Please let them be OK. She shook the water from her eyes and searched for her friends. 'Tash! Sierra!'

'*Elly?*'

It was Tash! She was nearby. Elly's heart gave a leap of pure relief as she saw Tash's blonde head appear, bobbing in the water above an orange life jacket. Her friend was pulling herself hand by hand around the dinghy. But what about Sierra? She had to be safe!

'Sierra!' Elly called. 'Sierra!'

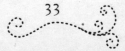

The only answer she got was the sound of Mojo yipping a greeting. Tash had attached Mojo to her with a rope, and the dog bobbed behind her, his life jacket keeping him safely afloat.

'Where's Sierra?' Elly called.

Tash shook her head, blinking back tears. 'I can't find her. We need to get the dinghy up. We can't help Sierra like this.'

Elly followed Tash as they fought their way back around to the other side of the capsized boat, facing the hull. Tash scooped Mojo up and held him under one arm. She gave Elly a pleading look. 'I have to hold him,' she explained. 'Even if it means working one armed. Otherwise, the dinghy might crush him when we right it.'

Elly nodded. Tash clambered onto the hull and managed to grab hold of the top edge of the boat with her free hand.

It was Elly's turn now. She climbed onto the

hull just as a wave sent the dinghy lurching upwards. She slipped off. Cold, salty water closed over her head and she swallowed a mouthful before her life jacket bobbed her above the waves again. But she was drifting away from the dinghy! She kicked frantically after the boat and managed to catch hold of it before the sea swept her away. Is that what had happened to Sierra? Was she floating, all alone, somewhere on that huge sea? Elly shuddered, fighting tears and panic. She couldn't fall apart now.

'Elly?' Tash was shouting over the noise of the sea and wind. 'Are you all right?'

Elly nodded, saving her breath, and shook  water out of her eyes. Just as she was about to try to climb onto the hull again, she spotted something moving towards her, swimming strongly through the waves.

'Sierra!' Elly
screamed, then
choked again as a
wave hit her in the face. By the time she had
stopped coughing, her friend had joined her
and was clinging to the boat's hull.

'Boy, am I glad to see you guys!' Sierra
gasped. 'I got swept away and nearly
couldn't find the boat again. I must have
swum in circles for a mile. And I nearly lost
my *handbag!*'

A huge grin of relief broke over Tash's face.
'Give me the details later. Now we've got to
save the *Mojo*. Help Elly get this boat right
side up. Just like we practised, OK?'

'That was in the harbour,' Sierra shouted
over the wind. 'The waves were tiny!'

'You can do it!' Tash called.

'Come on, let's go for it!' Elly was so
relieved to have Sierra back that she felt strong
enough to do anything. She watched for the

right moment, a breathing space between two large waves, and clambered onto the hull next to Tash. Sierra squeezed between them. Elly grabbed the edge of the boat with both hands. 'Ready!' she called to Tash.

'OK!' Tash said. 'Just like we practised. On three. One … two … THREE!'

Elly flung herself backwards with a yell, willing the *Mojo*'s mast to rise out of the sea. Beside her, Tash and Sierra were doing the same. For a long, tense moment it seemed as though they would fail, as the dinghy hung balanced, ready to fall either way. But then, with a sticky, reluctant tug, the sea loosened its grip and the *Mojo* righted itself. It floated, hull down, mast up.

Elly hung by her hands from the side, bobbing with the boat as it rose and sank on the surging waves. Tash had pulled herself up far

enough to drop Mojo safely inside. She heaved herself over the edge and turned to pull Sierra aboard. Then both of them reached for Elly. She scrabbled into the dinghy and landed in several inches of water. A solid, if soggy, floor beneath her feet had never felt so good!

Chapter 4

'I'll take the tiller!' Tash ran to take control of the boat once more. 'I can still steer a bit, even without sails.'

Elly joined Sierra in the bottom of the boat. They were sitting in six inches of water, but she was so wet it didn't matter. She peered out at the waves. The rain fell from the sky in solid sheets. She could only see a few feet and then the world disappeared behind a curtain of water. The waves looked oily black in the gloom of the storm.

'Can you take care of Mojo?' Tash called. The dog was crouched at her feet. 'I need to

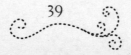

concentrate on avoiding rocks.'

Elly picked up the shivering dog. Mojo whimpered but let her sit with him cuddled on her lap. She held on to the anchor tackle with one hand and clutched Mojo to her with the other. He snuggled close to her for warmth and comfort and she pressed her face into his damp fur. Please let them all get safely to land!

Sierra screamed, and Elly's head jerked up. She and Tash spotted it at the same moment. The dark shape of a rock loomed out of the sea directly in front of them. Tash yelled and jammed the tiller hard to the left. The *Mojo* groaned and her bow lurched sickeningly to the right. Too terrified even to scream, Elly watched as the dinghy swept past the rock, missing by centimetres. She stared through the sheeting

rain and her straining eyes made out a large shadow, dead ahead. It grew more solid with every second. An island! And the *Mojo* was being driven straight at it.

'Tash!'

But Tash had already seen the danger. Rocks, jagged and sharp as sharks' teeth, reared out of the storm-lashed waves, eager to rip the *Mojo* to shreds. Elly's heart thudded in her ears, louder even than the howl of the wind. Tash grunted with effort as she fought the tiller, doing her best to guide the boat through the deadly maze.

With or without a sail, Elly thought, we can't turn the dinghy round in this storm. We're going to run aground. The thought made her stomach turn over.

Someone grabbed her arm and Elly turned her head to see Sierra's face, ghostly pale in the gloom. Her friend's brown eyes were huge with fear. Elly took hold of Sierra's cold hand

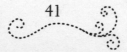

and squeezed it hard. Mojo whimpered. She held him tight with her free arm and secured herself as well as possible, bracing her body with her feet. Then she closed her eyes and waited.

The boat scraped and lurched, bouncing off rocks like a pinball. Tash worked the tiller in grim silence. The storm raged all around them. Rain pelted down. Elly had gone beyond fear now and felt oddly calm. She could feel Mojo shaking and sang softly to him. Her brain barely recognized the song: a lullaby that her mother used to sing to her when Elly was very little.

The dinghy leapt in the water and groaned like a living creature as it struck a rock full on. The little boat shuddered and Elly heard the sound of the hull ripping open. At the same moment, she was flung forward into the air and Mojo was thrown from her arms. Elly found herself rolling across the bottom of the dinghy, thumping into the sides of the boat and bits of tackle as the dinghy crashed into rocks again and again, then seemed to lift and slide up and over a barrier and onto something solid and unmoving. The boat listed onto its side and Elly felt herself falling. The next moment, she was lying face down in shallow water.

Elly pushed herself up, choking and spluttering. She sat back on her knees, waist deep in water, waves smacking into her back, sometimes crashing over her head. She shook with exhaustion as the adrenaline drained from her body.

I'm alive! She sat motionless in the water, getting her breath back and concentrating on that amazing thought. Another wave drenched her, and it felt like waking up from

a dream. She mustn't sit here in the water. She needed to get properly ashore. Elly climbed to her feet.

Blinking salt water from her eyes, she saw that she was on the foreshore of an island, crouching in half a metre of water on a sandy beach strewn with granite boulders. Next to her, the remains of the *Mojo* lay on its side like a stranded whale. Sierra was staggering to her feet nearby. Two safe! Elly clutched her friendship charm as she searched through the rain for any sign of Tash. She felt giddy with relief as she saw her friend knee-deep in the sea on the other side of the wrecked dinghy, holding onto its hull for support. They had all made it!

'Mojo!' Tash cried, and Elly didn't know for a moment if she meant the boat or the dog. Then something part orange and part dog-

coloured swam into sight just beyond the boat. Tash gathered her dog to her with a sob. Elly and Sierra splashed through the wind and waves to Tash and Mojo and the four of them stood for a moment, hugging each other tight while the waves and wind tried to knock them over.

'We're safe!' Sierra whooped. 'I almost can't believe it. Let's get onto solid land. I don't know about you, but I'm never getting into a boat again!'

They waded ashore. The rain was slackening. The sky was bright blue to the west beyond the band of dark clouds. The storm was passing.

'Quick, get these life jackets off.' Tash knelt and unbuckled Mojo. 'We'll dry sooner without them.'

Sierra slipped off her neon-pink armbands. 'Lot of good these did,' she said, deflating

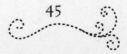

them. She gathered the life jackets and dumped them higher on the beach, anchoring them with rocks.

'The dinghy's safe there for the moment.' Tash stopped trying to dry off Mojo with her damp neck scarf and glanced back at the remains of her boat. Elly had known that Tash loved her dinghy, but she hadn't known how much until now. Tash looked ill. The *Mojo* had several deep gashes in its hull. Its fibreglass body was bashed and scraped and one whole section torn away. Elly wouldn't have recognized it as the boat they had started out in so happily only an hour ago.

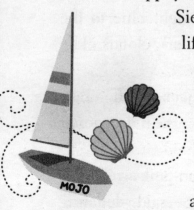

Sierra finished securing the life jackets and ran back to join them. She stumbled to a stop as she took in the state of the *Mojo*. 'Oh no! Tash! Your beautiful boat! I didn't mean it about boats, really. I love

the *Mojo*! It's a brave little dinghy. It got us to safety, and now look at it.' She looked ready to cry. 'Can it be fixed?'

'Maybe,' Tash said, surveying the remains of her boat with a grim face. 'But we're safe and that's what matters. Now, help me flip it over. I need to get to the radio.'

Elly stood between Tash and Sierra as they heaved at the dinghy and turned it upright. 'Euuw!' Sierra cried as the extent of the mess was revealed. 'Everything's smashed to bits.'

Even though she'd known it would be bad, Elly was shocked at the sight that met her eyes: broken floorboards, smashed tackle, tangled ropes. While Tash investigated the boat's radio, Sierra and Elly started to unpick the mess of ropes and torn canvas. Elly spotted the cargo bag that held her backpack. Her mouth felt drier than the sand. She scooped out her drinks bottle and took a swig.

Water had never tasted so good.

'I'd go easy on that, Elly.' Tash's voice was sharp.

Elly choked on her last swallow and looked up at her friend, standing in the stern of the boat beside the radio. Or what was left of it. Even from here Elly could see it was smashed beyond repair. She felt her face go blank with dismay. How would anyone know where they were?

'Mobile phones?' Sierra asked, in a too-bright voice. 'I...sort of dropped mine.'

'I've got mine.' Giddy relief made Elly giggle as she rooted through her backpack. Her fingers soon touched the smooth, familiar shape. She yanked the mobile out of her pack and waved it overhead like a trophy. 'Whoohoo! Elly to the rescue!'

'Try it,' Tash said, chewing

her lower lip.

'Oh.' Elly's heart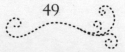
sank as she studied
her phone. 'No reception.
I should have known. Half the time I can't
even get any on Sunday Island.'

'That's why I always carry a short-wave.'
Tash stared at the mangled radio at her feet.
'But my sailing instructors never told me
what you do if your radio gets smashed to bits
along with your boat.' For a moment, totally-
in-command Tash looked scared. 'B-but it'll
be OK.'

'How?' Sierra's voice was rising decibel by
decibel. 'No one knows where we are!'

'Well...' Tash frowned in thought. 'Mum
knows we're whale watching today. I mean,
of course I told her what we were doing.'

'Well, I told my dad too,' Sierra snapped.
'Not that he'll have paid the slightest bit
of attention.'

'And I told Aunt Dina.' Elly was trying to

keep panic at bay. 'But she doesn't know which way we sailed. Did you tell your mum we were heading for the Western Isles, Tash?'

'I-I'm not sure. I really can't remember. I was in a hurry and she's always busy.' Tash looked as if she'd rather be anywhere else on earth. 'I messed up. I'm sorry. I'm the captain and it's my job to make sure we sail safely. It's just that I really wanted to be the first to find the whales. I was sure they'd be somewhere around these islands. And I was right. Elly saw a whale spout just before the storm struck.'

'Yeah. Great.' Sierra collapsed onto the bottom of the boat with a groan. 'So we're shipwrecked and no one knows where we are, but that's OK because we've got some whales for company. Just…great.'

Chapter 5

Tash's face was pink with guilt. 'I'm sorry. But this isn't the middle of nowhere. We're only a few miles from Sunday Island. Boats from the island and the mainland visit the Western Isles all the time in the summer, taking the tourists bird watching and seal spotting. We're bound to be picked up. We just need to make sure we get seen as soon as possible. Let's find out which island we've been shipwrecked on.'

Tash turned to Elly, her eyes sparkling with adventure again. 'Bring the binocs, Elly. Let's get up as high as we can and have a recce.' She headed off at a run, Mojo darting after her.

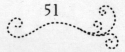

Elly put a hand to her chest. The binoculars were still there, hanging by their strap around her neck. She hadn't even noticed. Sierra, looking only slightly happier, had already started after Tash. Elly soon caught up. They scrambled up the granite headland cutting the cove off from the rest of the island. Elly had to use all her concentration to negotiate the huge granite rocks, which seemed to have been piled there by a giant long ago. She leapt and climbed from boulder to boulder, across crevices and occasional rock pools fringed with limpet shells.

By the time she had pulled herself to the top of the headland, Elly was hot and sweaty. She stood next to her friends on top of a huge boulder.

'Let me borrow the binocs,' Tash said, struggling to balance against the wind. She held them to her eyes

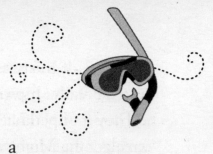

and scanned the sea around them. 'The storm blew us totally off course.' Tash turned in a slow circle, doing a 360 degree sweep. 'This should be Tash Island, but it isn't. It's over there.' She pointed to an island standing at least a mile to the east of them. Elly could see the large triangular shaped rock that made Tash Island unmistakable.

'So, where are we?' Sierra asked.

'Elly Island. And that,' Tash pointed to a small hill behind them, in the centre of their island, 'is the highest point on this island, so that's where we'll erect a rescue beacon. But first we need to do some salvaging and see what supplies we can gather from the *Mojo*.'

'And have lunch,' Sierra cried as they climbed back down the rocks. 'I'm starving!'

Elly felt a grin spread over her face as she clambered after her friends. It felt good to hear Sierra complaining about being hungry.

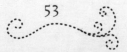

Almost as if this was a normal day and they weren't really shipwrecked at all.

They tramped back across the island to the wreck of the *Mojo*.

'Not a dream, then,' Elly muttered, looking at the broken mast and tangled sail.

'No, I'm afraid it's all too real.' Tash climbed into the dinghy. 'First things first: water and food. If we're really unlucky, we might be camping out tonight.'

'*What*?!' shrieked Sierra. 'No, we won't! That is totally unacceptable. I don't *do* camping. Not without hot water and showers. And TV! And…room service,' she moaned. Her eyes grew dreamy and wistful.

'You're thinking hotels, not campsites.' Elly was trying not to laugh. Sierra looked so tragic.

'Camping overnight isn't a big deal,' Tash said. 'But water is. There isn't

MOJO

a water supply on any of these islands, so that's the first priority.' She headed to the front of the boat to investigate the bow's storage area, then turned back to her friends with a wide grin on her face. 'We're in luck! I always carry fresh water on board and the jerrycan survived. We've got ten litres. Enough for ages. Plus what you guys are carrying in your bags.'

'Enough for a bath?' Sierra said hopefully.

'No!' Elly and Tash shouted together.

'You can always go for a swim,' Elly suggested.

'At least I've got sunblock in here.' Sierra collapsed on the beach with a sigh. She unzipped her handbag. Elly couldn't believe it had survived and everything inside was bone dry. 'Never doubt the handbag,' Sierra said when she noticed Elly starring. She fished in her handbag and pulled out a tube. When she'd finished putting on sunblock,

Sierra tossed the tube to Elly. 'Go on, guys, on with the suncream. You'll thank me when you're forty.'

Tash giggled, but she took the tube after Elly and smeared some on her face. 'You're right. I'll be burning already, and I forgot mine.'

'So water and skin care are sorted. What about food?' Sierra asked. 'I've only got a few sandwiches, three packets of crisps, two chocolate bars and a couple of apples. Hardly anything. Isn't it lunch time yet? I'm hungry.'

Elly bit her lip hard, trying not to laugh. 'It's only just after eight a.m., Sierra.'

Sierra tucked her hair behind both ears and wrinkled her nose in disbelief. 'It can't be.'

'Don't worry,' Elly soothed. 'Aunt Dina gave me a huge lunch. I've got enough sandwiches

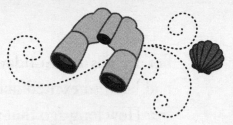

for everyone, plus fruit and three pieces of cake.'

'Your aunt's special chocolate marble orange cake?' Sierra was looking much more cheerful.

'Yup.'

'Well, it sounds like we've got water, skin care *and* food sorted.' Tash was looking quite pleased. Elly could tell that, now the danger was past, Tash was enjoying their adventure. 'We need to build a beacon so passing boats will know we're here.'

'Food first!' Sierra rubbed her stomach and stared at them mournfully. 'I've swum *miles*! Well,' she said, as Tash and Elly stared at her dubiously, 'it feels that way.'

They picnicked high up on the beach, sitting side by side in the sand, leaning against a boulder and stretching their legs out in the sun. Elly suddenly felt exhausted. Only a few hours had passed since she had stood with

her friends on Sunday Island beach. They had been so excited about their adventure at sea. How long ago that seemed.

She stared out to sea. It was transformed from the furious beast that had tried to kill them. The sky was cloudless and the sun bounced and played on the tops of the waves, glinting off them in iridescent sparks. The wind had dropped to a gentle breeze and the view in front of her, white sand and blue sea, was postcard perfect. It was almost impossible to believe that they were really and truly shipwrecked. Just like an Edith Builtmore book, she thought. How strange, and rather wonderful.

'Food!' Sierra ordered, pointing to Elly's backpack.

Elly explored the lunch Aunt Dina had packed. As usual, her aunt had

supplied five times
more food than Elly
could eat by herself.
She decided the cheese
and pickle sandwiches would last longest in
the summer heat, so she handed everyone a
ham roll, an apple, and a thick slice of cake.
Tash immediately fed most of her sandwich
to Mojo, who was whining hopefully.

'I'm not that hungry,' she said. But from the
way Tash attacked her apple and cake, Elly
could tell she was lying. Mojo still seemed
hungry, so Elly fished a piece of ham out of
her roll and held it out for the border terrier,
who snapped it up and then kept his large
brown eyes trained on every mouthful she
took after that.

'Don't even look at me,' Sierra told the dog.
She wolfed down her roll at record speed. As
she was about to take the last bite, Mojo gave
a mournful sigh. 'Oh, all right.' Sierra tossed
it to the dog instead. 'You had better enjoy

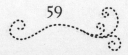

that,' she called as she picked up her apple and took a juicy bite.

Elly munched her own apple, watching the waves lapping the stranded dinghy. The sound of the water, beating gently against the boat, was almost hypnotic. But the rhythmic sound gave her a sudden pang of loneliness. Thank goodness Tash and Sierra were here too.

'We'll pull the *Mojo* further up the beach in a minute,' Tash said, noticing where Elly was looking. 'If we don't get rescued today we could sleep in the boat.'

'We're going to be rescued,' Sierra said firmly, around her last mouthful of chocolate and orange cake. 'That was yum! What's next, boss?'

'To eat or to do?' asked Elly with a wicked grin.

'Hey! I do think about other things besides food.'

'Absolutely,' Tash said, her face straight. 'You think about clothes too.'

Sierra pelted her with sand.

'Hey! I'm counting on you and your handbag.' Tash brushed sand from her blonde spikes. 'Don't tell me you didn't bring a change of clothes or a towel or something.'

'What do you want it for?' Sierra looked suspicious.

'A flag, of course.'

'You're not using my best sarong for a flag.' Sierra's brown eyes snapped with outrage.

'Well, I guess you'll be sleeping in the boat tonight.' Tash shrugged. 'Shame the mosquitoes are so bad this time of year.'

'Oh, all right.' Grumbling, Sierra dug around in her handbag and pulled out an enormous purple sarong with acid green stripes. She handed it, neatly folded, to Tash. 'Be careful with it.'

'Wow.' Elly looked at the garment with awe.

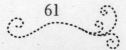

'You really…wear that?'

'Almost as good as neon pink armbands.' Tash grinned and got to her feet.

'Just because you're fashion challenged,' Sierra spluttered.

'I bow to you, O Supreme Fashionista!' Tash waved the sarong in surrender. 'After all, you brought this marvellous flag…uh, I mean sarong. Now, help me pull the *Mojo* up the beach, then let's look for some driftwood for a flagpole.'

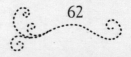

Chapter 6

'What this island needs is a tree,' Elly said half an hour later, as she lugged her third backpackful of heavy granite pebbles from the beach up the small hill that formed the centre of the island. They had found a three metre piece of planking washed ashore and dragged it to the highest point on the island. Then all three of them had collected rocks to pile around the base of the plank to hold it upright.

'That should do it,' Tash groaned as she dumped the last of her pebbles from a canvas bag.

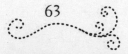

'I hope so.' Sierra frowned at her hands. 'I forgot to bring nail varnish.'

'Time for the flag.' Tash whipped the sarong from around her waist, where she had tied it for safe-keeping, and knelt to tie it onto the flagpole, using bits of rope she had salvaged from the *Mojo*. 'All done! Let's lift it up and use the rocks to hold it.'

Sierra held the flagpole steady as Tash and Elly piled the rocks around the base of the plank. When she ran out of rocks, Elly jumped back to take a look. The purple and green sarong flapped in the steady breeze. 'It's certainly bright enough. Thanks, Sierra.'

'Hmm.' Sierra frowned at her beachwear. 'It had better work. I don't sacrifice my best clothes lightly, you know.'

'Someone is bound to see it. You get a really good view from up

here.' Elly had the
binoculars. She lifted
them to her eyes and
scanned the sea between Elly Island and the
distant outline of Sunday Island. 'But I don't
see any boats yet.'

'No.' Sierra gazed back towards the low
greenish-grey mound that was Sunday Island.
'It looks ever so far away.'

Elly turned towards open sea. At first she
couldn't believe what she was seeing. Then
she caught her breath. It was real. 'Look!
The whales!'

'Where?'

She handed the binoculars to Tash, who
was jumping up and down madly. Elly didn't
really need them to see the animals. They
were swimming near the mouth of a cove on
the north-east side of Elly Island, two rounded
backs surging slowly through the water, one
large and one much smaller. 'Oh wow,' Elly
said. 'It looks like a mother and baby whale.'

'Oh, how gorgeous,' Sierra gasped. 'What I wouldn't give for a camera now. We'd be sure to win. Have you got yours, Tash?'

'No, I lost it in the storm.' Tash kept the binoculars trained on the whales. 'Oh no!' she cried. 'This isn't good!'

The sound of her voice made Elly turn to stare at her friend. 'What's wrong?'

Tash lowered the binoculars. Her face looked worried. 'See that line of rocks sticking out of the water just beyond the bay? That's the upper edge of the canyon I was telling you about. The mother whale is outside those rocks, but the baby is inside. I don't think it can find its way through to its mum and the tide is going out.'

'Can't it just wait until the tide comes back in?' Sierra asked.

'No, it's getting upset and swimming further into

the cove. It could get stranded. You know, stuck on the beach. It won't be able to breathe. Without water to hold it up, it will be suffocated by its own weight.'

Elly watched the two whales, one large, one small. A mother and child. A hot, aching lump filled her throat. Just a few months ago, she'd lost her mum to cancer. She couldn't stand by and let the whale and its baby lose each other. 'We've got to do something!' she cried.

'Maybe we can save it.' Tash began to run down the hill towards the whales. 'Come on!'

Elly sprinted after her. She was the fastest runner of the three and she soon overtook Tash. Even Sierra's long legs couldn't keep up. It was a wild scramble down the hillside. There was no path and Elly had to dodge prickly gorse bushes and detour around granite outcrops. Finally she reached the

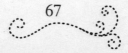

rocky foreshore that led to the small beach. She slipped and slid over boulders slimy with seaweed and jumped over rock pools.

Sierra piled into her and grabbed Elly around the shoulders to keep herself upright. 'Tash was right,' Elly said. 'The baby's heading straight for us. It's nearly aground already.' She turned and gestured impatiently to Tash, who was following Mojo down the last of the rocks. Tash spotted the baby whale and pelted across the beach, Mojo at her heels. She skidded to a stop, puffing and holding her sides. Mojo's ears pricked up and he barked in surprise at the sight of the whale calf as it surged and struggled in the tiny cove, making high-pitched squeaking and clicking noises. The dog barked eagerly, wagging his tail and frisking at the edge of the waves.

'Sorry, Mojo,' Tash panted. 'It can't play

with you right now.'

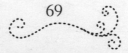

The calf was much bigger close up. It looked nearly as big as a dinghy. It had smooth dark grey skin and a dolphin-like head and nose. It was thrashing its head about and making frightened squeaking noises. Elly could hear the mother whale's reply from beyond the barrier of rocks: a series of clicks and whistles, growing louder and more frantic.

Tash waded knee-deep in the bay, studying the calf and the tide. 'We have to turn that calf round and guide it back out past the barrier to open sea.' She kept pushing her hair off her forehead, making it spikier than ever. Elly could tell she was working hard to keep calm. 'But it's already halfway to beaching itself. We can't just lift it off. It may look small compared to its mum, but it'll be over three metres long and very heavy. We need ideas. Quick!'

'A raft!' Elly cried. 'Do you remember

when that whale swam up the Thames a few years ago? It got trapped and couldn't find its way out of the river back to sea. Mum and I watched the rescue attempt on TV. They floated it on a raft.'

'But we haven't got a raft,' Tash said, her eyes never leaving the whale calf, which was splashing and whistling in distress.

'Life jackets!' Elly had a flash of inspiration. 'We've got four life jackets.'

'Genius!' Tash shouted, then clamped a hand over her mouth as the noise seemed to upset the whale even more. 'And there are a couple of those big cushions that act as floatation devices stowed under the bow. You're the fastest runner, Elly. There's a small pocket knife in the cargo bag just to the right of the tiller. Gather all the stuff and cut as much rope as you can from the rigging. Then bring everything back here. Sierra and I have got to try to calm that calf down before it injures itself.'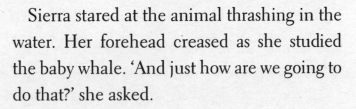

Sierra stared at the animal thrashing in the water. Her forehead creased as she studied the baby whale. 'And just how are we going to do that?' she asked.

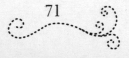

Chapter 7

Elly didn't wait to hear the answer. She set off at her fastest pace. It was a long, hard run back to the dinghy. She found the knife and cut several long lengths of rope. She scrambled to the bow to get the cushions, slipped on something and nearly fell. She knelt and picked up the soggy remains of the Edith Builtmore book. It was a mess: wet through and the cloth cover torn. Elly pulled out the cushions and put the book in their place. She still wanted to read it, but even Edith Builtmore couldn't have imagined anything as exciting as her own island adventure. She

just hoped it would have a happy ending for the whales.

Elly gathered up cushions and rope and grabbed the life jackets off the beach. She staggered back to the whale cove with her arms piled so high she could barely trot. She was sweating and totally out of breath by the time she climbed down the rocky slope to the beach.

Tash jogged across the sand to meet her. 'Sierra's got a new talent,' she said, a wide grin on her face as she took the cushions and rope from Elly.

'What?' Elly peered past Tash and saw an amazing sight. Mojo sat on the shore, motionless except for pointed, swivelling ears. He watched the baby whale intently, but it was Sierra who made Elly's mouth drop open. Sierra stood chest deep in

the water facing the
baby whale. She was
so close she could
have reached out and
touched it. And she was singing!

'She's a whale whisperer,' Tash announced
triumphantly. 'We tried everything. Talking
to it, making soothing noises, doing the
"ommm" thing from yoga. And then Sierra
tried singing and it worked.'

The calf lay still in the water and seemed to
be watching Sierra as she sang to it in Spanish.

'The tide's still going out,' Tash said,
suddenly brisk again. 'No time to lose.'

They knelt in the sand and tied the two
large cushions together along one side to
form the middle of the raft, then fastened
the life jackets around all four sides. Mojo
came to help, sticking his whiskery muzzle
into everything, tail wagging with delight.
Elly watched Tash's fingers twist and twirl the
rope into complicated knots as quickly and

deftly as a magician making toy animals out of balloons. 'How do you *do* that?'

'Sailor stuff,' Tash said. 'Can't sail without knowing your knots.'

Elly glanced back at the receding tide. It was still flowing out of the bay and Sierra was only waist deep in the water now. 'I hope you're nearly finished. We need to get this whale back to its mum now.'

'Sorted!' Tash tugged on each of the ropes, testing her knots. 'Making the raft was the easy bit. I just hope this works.'

Elly and Tash dragged the life jacket raft over the beach to the water's edge. Mojo gave a little yip of excitement, and Sierra stopped singing for a moment to see what was happening. Immediately the whale began to thrash in the water, twisting its bottle-nosed snout back and forth, whistling and clicking.

'Sing!' Elly and Tash cried together.

Sierra nodded and started singing again. Her voice was hoarse and croaky, but the calf calmed at once. Sierra waved frantically at them as she sang, pointing at the tide line inching steadily out to sea.

Carefully and slowly, so as not to frighten it, Elly and Tash floated the raft towards the baby whale. They stopped a metre or two away and let the calf give the raft a long curious look and poke at it with its snout. Mojo had been watching the whale intently, wagging his tail and whining. Now he plunged into the water and dog-paddled towards the raft, dark head bobbing, front paws splashing.

'Mojo! No!' Tash ordered. 'Go back to the beach before you scare the calf.'

'Wait,' Elly said. 'It likes him.'

The whale calf watched Mojo approach with bright eyes, making a soft clicking noise.

When Mojo got close enough, it reached out its nose and gave the dog a gentle nudge. Mojo yelped in surprise and paddled quickly to Tash, who picked him up with a laugh.

'Yes, it's big. Now go back to the beach and wait. This is no place for little dogs.' She hauled Mojo back to the beach and deposited him on the sand. 'Stay.' Tash's voice was stern and the border terrier seemed to sense that she meant business. He lay down on the sand and put his head on his paws. Tash waded back towards them. Sierra sang on, her voice a husky whisper.

Mojo's visit had somehow calmed the calf, Elly thought. Its large round eye watched her, then turned towards Sierra. It seemed happy to have them and the raft close beside it now. 'They're very intelligent animals,' Tash said in a whisper, joining Elly and

MOJO

grabbing hold of the raft again. 'They like to play. And they're not really frightened of humans, so let's see if it will let us slide this under its belly and use it to push it back into deeper water. Then we can get the raft more securely underneath it and guide the baby around the breakers and back to her mum.'

At Tash's signal, Elly edged closer to the whale. The water lapped at her waist now, comfortably warm through the wetsuit. How amazing to be this close to a whale! she thought. Her heart was banging in her chest with excitement. The calf's skin was dark, glossy and smooth, unlike anything she had ever seen before. She looked into the bright, intelligent eye facing them and knew she would do everything she could to save this animal.

Sierra continued to sing the same song,

over and over. She croaked worse than ever now, but the tune was low and sweet. Elly caught herself humming along and wondered what the words meant. Was it some sort of Spanish lullaby?

The calf nudged the raft, then lifted its beak and chittered. It sounded almost happy. Tash nodded at Elly and, standing one on either side of the whale's head, they gently pushed the raft under water and guided it beneath the front of the calf's belly.

When the raft touched the whale, it jerked and whistled in alarm, but Sierra sang louder and after a moment it calmed down and let the girls continue to work the raft beneath its tummy.

'It seems to be working.' Tash's voice was an excited whisper. 'We're floating it higher in the water.'

She was right. The raft

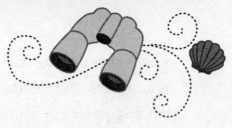

was lifting the
front of the calf
off the seabed.

'Gently does it!'
Tash said. They continued
to work the raft beneath the whale. 'That's
enough, I think.' Tash's eyes shone with
excitement. 'Come on, guys. Elly and Sierra,
you stay on that side. I'll stay on this. We're
going to push it back out into the bay and
then swim it on the raft around those rocks
to Mum.'

Elly was too nervous to speak. She nodded,
as did Sierra, still singing away. They each took
firm hold of the edges of the raft, anchored
their feet and, at Tash's command, began to
push. Nothing happened. Oh no! Elly felt
panic sweep over her. What if the whale was
too heavy? She remembered how sad she and
her mum had been when the whale in the
Thames finally died, despite all the scientists
and volunteers tried to do to help save it.

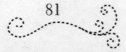

That wasn't going to happen to her whale! She gritted her teeth and pushed with all her might.

The raft moved. A few centimetres, and then more, and then suddenly it shot away from the shore. Taken by surprise, Elly lost her grip and fell face down into the water. She surfaced, gasping and spluttering. Sierra and Tash had managed to hold on and were kicking through the water, guiding the whale raft towards the mouth of the cove. Elly plunged after them, swimming strongly, and soon caught up.

It was hard work, swimming while pushing the raft. Tash stopped every few moments to make sure they were on course. If Sierra stopped singing to catch her breath the baby whale whistled in distress. Elly heard the mother whale becoming more and

more agitated on
the other side of
the breakers. She
seemed to be following
them, keeping pace as they floated the calf
out of the cove and into the stretch of water
between the island and the underwater ridge.
The baby whale seemed to know what they
were doing. At any rate, it kept quite still on
the raft. The water was growing choppier as
they neared open sea, and Elly's arms and
legs were getting tired.

'Nearly there!' Tash called encouragement.
Elly realized that this was probably Tash's
dream moment: being so close to the whales
she loved and actually helping to save one.

Suddenly it felt as if someone had turned on
the cold tap. Waves charged down on them,
higher and stronger. They had reached the
end of the barrier of rocks. A spout of water
shot into the air right in front of them. The
mother whale surfaced. She called to her

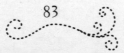

baby with whistles, clicks and grunts. With one wriggle of its sleek body, the calf slid off the raft and ploughed through the waves towards its mother.

Now instead of pushing a heavy weight through the water, Elly was bobbing up and down holding one edge of the makeshift raft. Sierra and Tash bobbed beside her.

The mother whale nuzzled its baby, grunting softly. The two animals circled each other, then swam slowly towards open sea, so close together they were nearly touching. Elly watched them go. She struggled not to cry. Lucky calf! It had lost its mother but found her again. The pain of missing her own mother washed through her.

It never seemed to hurt less—she just got more used to it each day.

Mum would be proud of me, she told herself. Elly watched as

the whales arched their
backs and dived beneath
the waves with a flip of
their huge tails. Then she
turned and swam with the others back to the
beach, where Mojo was barking goodbye to
his new friend.

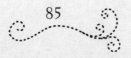

Chapter 8

'What was that song you were singing to the whale?' Elly asked. The girls lay stretched out on the beach, letting the sun warm them up and getting their breath back. Elly felt like a wobbly jelly inside when she thought of the amazing thing they had just done. 'Was it a Spanish lullaby? It sounded sweet.'

Sierra sat up, looking pink and embarrassed. Sierra? Embarrassed?

Elly sat up too, sensing a mystery. 'Come on, spill!'

'Uh...it wasn't a lullaby.' Sierra was definitely blushing. 'It's a song my dad sings

sometimes when he's had a bit of wine. About falling in love. He said he used to sing it to my mother.'

Elly laughed. 'Well, the mother whale and her baby love each other, so that's all right.'

Elly glanced at Tash, expecting to see her grinning at the idea of Sierra singing a love song to a whale, but their friend was staring at a pile of driftwood and frowning. 'What's up, Tash?'

Tash sat up and stretched. 'The storm threw up so much stuff. You wouldn't expect to see all that rubbish washed onto one beach after a storm.' She leapt to her feet and began to walk up and down the beach, pulling things out of the heaps of debris the storm had washed ashore and piling some of them together.

'What *is* she doing?'

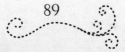

Sierra watched Tash squat down beside a plank of wood and stare at it. 'Uh oh. I think the captain's gone loopy. Prepare to mutiny, crew!'

'Hey, come and look at this!' Tash waved them over.

Elly jogged over to Tash and squatted beside her. Sierra plopped down on the sand and draped an arm over Tash's shoulders. 'Too much sun? Bump your head in the capsize?'

Tash ignored the teasing, her face intent. She gestured at the pile of wood she had collected. 'This is all part of an old ship. That storm must have dislodged a wreck and brought some of it up to the surface.' She handed a short piece of planking to Elly and one to Sierra, who wrinkled her nose as she took it. A fur of rotting seaweed clung to the wood.

'There are barnacles growing on it. Some of them pretty big. It's been under water for a while.' Tash sounded excited. 'And look at this.' She held out a piece of wood which had some faded blue paint on one side and something written in large white letters:

••• **more Adv** •••

'A shipwreck?' Sierra frowned at the wood she was holding. 'Do you mean it's wrecked near here?' She didn't sound happy at the idea.

Elly glanced at the cove. Somewhere under those calm waves lay a boat that had carried people. Just as the *Mojo* had carried them today. What had happened to the unknown boat and its crew?

'Must be.' Tash jumped to her feet and looked out towards the sea. 'Probably hit those breakers. I bet it's in the canyon. I told you, the Western Isles are death traps for ships in a storm.'

'But that's awful.' Sierra dropped the

piece of planking on the sand as though it had burnt her. 'Those poor people, fighting the sea. We know how it feels.' Sierra stared out at the calm waters in the cove. She tucked a strand of hair slowly behind one ear, her face pensive.

'They might have survived,' Elly said.

'That's true,' said Tash. 'Lots of times fishermen are able to rescue people in shipwrecks off Sunday Island. They row out in fishing boats to save them. Maybe all the people on that boat were saved. But ...' She paused for dramatic effect. 'Maybe they had to leave their treasure behind.'

'Treasure?' Sierra's face changed. She glanced at the plank of wood Tash was holding with awe.

'What sort of treasure?' Elly asked, playing along with Tash. Pirate treasure didn't happen in real life, but it was fun to pretend.

'Gold? Jewels?'

'Well, it could have been a pirate ship.' Tash's eyes sparkled. 'Or a smuggler! There were both pirates and smugglers around here in the old days. Valuable stuff could still be on the wreck, or even buried somewhere on this island.'

'Pirates' treasure!' Elly was almost starting to believe in it now. 'This is just like one of my mum's movies. Those pirates buried the treasure on an island. On a beach just like this. Oh, except it had palm trees. I vote we start looking.'

'Um ...' Sierra put her hand up. 'I really hate to be the sensible one here. But we haven't got anything to dig with and we don't know where to dig. No "X-marks-the-spot"! You planning on digging up every inch of this island?'

Elly's shoulders slumped as her excitement faded. 'Oh.'

'Anyway, I for one want to get home and sleep in my own bed tonight and not in a wrecked dinghy with loads of mosquitoes for company.' Sierra jumped to her feet. 'We can come back another time and look for treasure maybe. Can I borrow some of this wood?'

'Sure.' Tash said. Her eyebrows crunched together in confusion. 'But what do you want it for?'

'Watch!' Sierra gathered the largest pieces of planking and driftwood. She placed them one next to the other in a pattern across the upper half of the beach.

Elly squinted at the shapes in the sand. Letters! 'H...E...L... She's spelling "HELP!"'

Sierra stood back, hands on hips, looking at her creation with a satisfied smile. 'Like in disaster films,' she explained. 'For when they

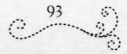

send the aeroplanes and helicopters to look for us.'

'Good idea,' Tash said. 'And while we're waiting to be rescued, I vote we do some underwater exploring. I'm not giving up on treasure just yet. Sierra, have you still got the snorkelling gear?'

Sierra dug the masks and snorkels out of her bag and handed them round. 'See. My handbag rules!'

'I'll never disrespect the handbag again,' Tash said, taking one set of snorkelling gear.

If only someone knew where they were, this would be a perfect day, Elly thought, as she waded out into the gentle waves of the cove with her friends. Mojo barked, and Elly turned to see him standing at the water's edge, wagging his tail mournfully.

'Stay, Mojo!' ordered Tash.

Elly hesitated, watching

MOJO

the other girls wading out into the cove. The sky was a hot, bright blue; seagulls and cormorants skimmed above a cobalt and turquoise sea. Tash and Sierra dived head-first into the waves. Elly glanced back at the white half-moon of sand fringing the cove. Surely it would be OK to explore, just for a little while. How often could she say she was searching for a shipwreck and buried treasure? They needed the distraction until someone spotted their flag. She adjusted the mask over her face and launched herself into the cool water.

Elly kicked hard, swimming strongly as she followed Tash and Sierra out of the cove towards the breakers. She caught up with them as they began to circle carefully around the jagged ridge of rocks. The water was cooler on the ocean side but the currents were gentle. After the fierce storm, the sea

seemed content to laze beneath a hot sun.

Once they had cleared the breakers, Tash stopped swimming and trod water, gazing around as though taking her bearings. Then she nodded and pointed to a spot a few metres ahead of them. 'I know the tides and currents around these islands,' she said. 'If there's a wreck, it's probably in this area. Snorkels on. The seabed isn't too deep here, even in the canyon. It's more of a gully really. Make sure you can always see the other two. And if you dive, surface in plenty of time, before you're desperate for air.'

Elly put the snorkel mouthpiece in her mouth, blew to clear it, then took a deep breath and dived. She had snorkelled on holiday with her cousins in the West Indies, but she had never seen an underwater world quite

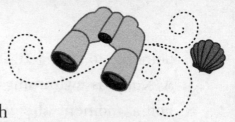

like this before.
The water around
her had turned greyish
blue and the sun was a bright yellow spot in an
undulating turquoise 'sky'. The seabed sloped
gently to form a shallow underwater canyon.
She swam above the canyon floor, in between
Tash and Sierra. Grey granite boulders
sprouted clumps of swaying seaweed. Coral
grew everywhere, shaped like miniature
cauliflowers and coloured white, tan and
pinkish grey. Colonies of sea anemones
waved their tentacles in the current. Fish
swam beside and beneath the girls, totally
unworried by their presence. Tash pointed at
an enormous lobster crawling along the sea
floor like some sort of prehistoric monster.

The girls surfaced for air, blowing water
out of their snorkels like porpoises before
diving again. Elly spotted a starfish creeping
along the seabed and tiny crabs scuttling
everywhere. Sierra touched her on the arm,

pointing to the left. Elly's heart lurched. A seal was swimming right towards them! For a moment she was scared: this close the animal seemed huge. Then she forgot to be nervous as she watched the seal, dark and water-sleeked, circle them gracefully, as though demonstrating how to swim properly. Its large, mournful eyes gazed at them. I will never forget this moment, Elly thought.

The sun's rays penetrated further as midday approached, turning the water all around them bright turquoise. The seal seemed to be fascinated by them. It kept swimming up to them, circling, swimming a bit further into the canyon, then coming back.

'It's almost as though it wants us to follow it,' Tash said, when they next surfaced for air. 'Let's see what happens if we do. Maybe it wants us to help it fish.'

'I'm not catching raw fish in my mouth,' Sierra said with a shudder.

'Just as well. You'd eat up all the seal's supper.' Tash laughed.

The seal was waiting for them when they went under water again. This time when it swam away Tash shot after it. Elly hesitated, then joined her and Sierra. It seemed a bit spooky, but after all, if she hadn't followed Mojo that first time back on Sunday Island, she would never have met Sierra and Tash.

They swam fifty or so metres westwards along the canyon, keeping just below the surface of the water and breathing through their snorkels. Then the seal, swimming a metre below, suddenly dived towards the canyon floor.

Elly squinted to see where it had gone and spotted something glinting in the depths, in the middle of a seaweed covered heap of what

 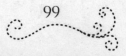

appeared to be rubbish. She tapped Tash on the leg and pointed at it. Tash took one look, nodded, and made the signal to surface. They kicked upwards and spat the mouthpieces out so they could talk.

'Definitely something down there,' Tash said, treading water. 'About five or six metres below the surface, so not too deep. Let's go have a look, but be careful about getting tangled in any wreckage. Stay well clear. Agreed?'

Elly and Sierra nodded. Elly took a giant lungful of air. She was shivering with excitement as she prepared to dive. Had they just found a pirate ship?

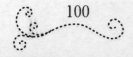

Chapter 9

Down and down Elly kicked through the greeny-blue water, past drifts of seaweed and clumps of coral. The sun angled strongly into the shallow canyon now, and Elly spotted the glimmer almost at once. Something metallic. But silver rather than the dull gold of a half-rotten chest full of doubloons. It came from the middle of a large dark shape lying on the sea floor.

In a few moments they had reached it. Elly's heart leapt as she saw the wooden ribs of a boat, covered in algae, barnacles and stranding seaweed. Fish swam slowly in and

out between them. It was a wrecked ship! She looked for what had glinted and saw ...a rusting outboard motor. And there: the aluminium fittings of a modern mast. Beside it lay a tangle of corroded chrome railings. The cabin lay in the middle of it all, still intact but coated with a thick layer of algae. So much for their pirate ship. This was the remains of a modern yacht. Tash pointed up to the surface. Time to get air. And give up on the dream of pirate treasure.

Tash lifted her mask. 'I was right,' Tash said. 'A real shipwreck! How amazing is that?' She was almost breathless with excitement. 'I want to go back down and take another look.'

'What are you looking for?' Elly suddenly felt that Tash wasn't telling them everything.

'Just a scout around. You guys stay here. I'll be

MOJO

back in a moment.'
Tash pulled on her
mask, and dived
before Elly could
stop her.

Sierra waved at Elly to get her attention
and pointed to the spot where Tash had
disappeared. Sierra was right. They couldn't
let her dive alone. Elly took a huge breath,
and followed Sierra in a deep dive.

The seal reappeared, keeping its distance
this time but following them as they swam
back to the wreck. Looking down through
the shimmering water at the bones of the old
boat, Elly thought it looked timeless and…
somehow sad. It was the same sort of feeling
old photographs gave her, or the funny old
black and white movies her mum had liked
to watch.

Something moved beside the wreck. Elly
spotted Tash circling the yacht's cabin, which
looked weirdly untouched by the disaster that

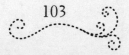

had struck the boat. As Elly watched, Tash pushed on the remains of the door. It opened, and to Elly's horror, Tash swam inside. Elly was after her like a shot, following a dolphin-quick Sierra. Tash was breaking her own rules.

They were at the cabin in seconds. They paused outside the door. What should they do? Follow Tash inside, even though it went against everything they had been told? Elly banged on the cabin wall. But her lungs were aching. She needed to go up for air. She caught Sierra's arm and pointed up. Her friend nodded. Sierra turned and thumped on the cabin with her fist.

Elly hesitated, her lungs on fire. She needed to swim for the surface, but she couldn't abandon her friends. What if Tash was trapped in there? Elly's chest felt as if it was going to explode. She had to

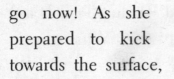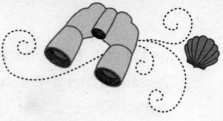

go now! As she prepared to kick towards the surface, Tash poked her head out of the cabin doorway. Elly saw Sierra grab Tash's arm and yank her towards the surface. She followed, relief flooding through her as she broke into the air to find her friends treading water, safe.

'Of all the stupid…' Sierra started but was too angry to finish. 'What were you thinking?' Elly gasped for breath, looking on in awe as Sierra let rip. 'Don't touch, you said! Stay clear in case it's dangerous. And you just swim right inside? We're not wearing scuba gear in case you hadn't noticed. You only have the air in your lungs.'

Tash trod water calmly, waiting for Sierra to finish. 'You're absolutely right. And you're right to be angry too,' she said, when Sierra finally spluttered to a halt. 'But I'm going to go in one last time.'

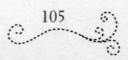

'What?!' Elly blurted. Hadn't Tash heard anything Sierra had just said? What was up with her?

'Let me finish,' said Tash. 'I spotted something in there I need to get. It's an easy grab—in and out. The cabin is safe. No ropes or wreckage to tangle me up. I'll do it on my own if I have to, but I'd rather you guys came along as backup.'

Sierra stared at Tash then turned to Elly, her face comic with dismay. 'She's mad.'

Elly hesitated. What could Tash possibly want so badly? Her friend was adventurous, but she wasn't reckless. It came down to this: did she trust Tash? Friends stuck together and looked after each other. Like they had done when Tash got trapped in the cave at Mirror Cove. And she'd been right then about finding their mothers' treasure. Tash

wouldn't do this unless it was really important.

Elly looked from Tash—bobbing up and down in the waves, her blonde hair plastered to her head and her nose turning pink in the sun—to Sierra, who was still shaking her head in amazement. 'OK,' Elly said. 'One last dive, then that's it. Whether you get this thing or not. Do you agree, Sierra?'

Sierra nodded. '*If* she promises.'

'I swear,' Tash said.

In a flash, she was gone. Elly dived after, Sierra swimming beside her. She watched as Tash darted into the cabin, and began unconsciously to count the seconds. Two... three...four...five...six...seven. Why was it taking so long? She glanced at Sierra in alarm, but her friend was watching the wreck intently. Elly glimpsed a black wetsuit and blonde hair; Tash emerged from the cabin.

She was swimming awkwardly, holding a sort of briefcase-shaped box by its handle. What had Tash found? All three of them kicked upwards.

As Elly surfaced, she heard Mojo barking frantically. Tash took off at once back towards the cove, Sierra following and soon taking the lead. But Elly heard something else out at sea. A motor! Rescue!

She turned and swam furiously towards the sound, past a headland of rocks, just in time to see one of Sunday Island's tourist sightseeing boats U-turn in the water and speed away, sending spray flying. Elly shouted and waved but it was no good. Her heart sank and she felt like crying. They hadn't seen her. But surely they must have seen the flag?

She twisted in the water and looked back at Elly Island. The flag was gone!

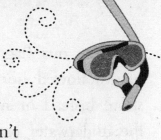

It was a long, slow swim back to the beach. Tash ran forward to help her out of the water. 'I don't know what he was fussing about.' She pointed to Mojo, who was now sitting on the sand next to Sierra, looking very happy to have his ears rubbed.

'I do,' Elly said, and threw herself down next to Sierra. She lay back on the warm sand with a groan. They had been so close to rescue. And it didn't help that every muscle in her body seemed to be screaming *enough already*! She sighed. Might as well get the bad news over. 'There was a motor boat. Mojo heard it. I swam out to try to wave them down but they'd already turned around.'

'*What*?' Sierra shot off the sand. 'Where? Where? Let's wave at them...start a fire...I don't know!'

'It's gone,' Elly snapped. She was feeling low. Their first chance of rescue was gone.

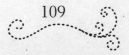

'Just like our flag.' She knew she should have followed her instinct and stayed on shore instead of swimming out to explore the underwater canyon. Treasure hunting! Some treasure.

'What? The flag's gone?' This time it was Tash who jumped to her feet. She darted up the beach in the direction of the flag. Five minutes later she was back, carrying a bedraggled purple and green sarong. 'The flagpole blew over.' She sank down beside them dejectedly.

'Argh!' Sierra grabbed the sarong and held it up. Great gashes were torn down its middle. 'It's ruined.'

'It blew away and caught on some bushes,' Tash said. 'And…um…there were some seagulls trying to steal it. You might want to rinse it off in case of… you know.'

MOJO

'Euew!' Sierra tossed the sarong away.

'I'll remake the flagpole,' Tash said. 'It's still the best chance we've got. Just need to engineer it stronger. Use some of the rigging for guy ropes.' Her voice petered out and she stared at the sand, digging at it with a finger. 'I keep thinking…'

'Yeah?' Elly asked, rolling over to watch her friend. Tash sounded sad, and worried. And neither of those were Tash-things.

'That yacht down there. It could so easily have been us.'

The fear and panic from when *their* ship was crashing came flooding back. Elly couldn't think of anything to say. Tash was right.

'I thought that too,' Sierra said. 'It was bad enough when I thought it was an old ship. Knowing it was modern makes it worse, somehow.' She shivered.

'But it wasn't us. We're fine,' Elly said.

Time to cheer herself and everyone else up.
'We're having an adventure right out of one
of Edith Builtmore's books. And we know it's
only a matter of time before someone comes
to find us.'

Sierra nodded, looking happier. 'Lunch?'
she asked hopefully.

'Lunch!' Tash agreed. 'But first: buried
treasure! I'm dying to know what was in that
box I found in the wreckage.'

In all the excitement, Elly had nearly
forgotten about the box Tash had salvaged
from the sunken yacht. What had been buried
under the sea for so long? Elly felt the tingle
of a mystery.

'Oh no you don't!'
Sierra exclaimed. 'Food
first, then treasure.
It's only fair,' she
added, when Tash
opened her mouth to
protest. 'We let you go

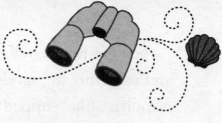

back into the wreck and all that extra swimming has made me hungry enough to eat raw seaweed.' She clutched her stomach. 'I'm starving!'

'Me too,' Elly said, smiling at Tash's look of dismay. 'I need food. Aunt Dina always says anticipation of something nice is always the best part. So we'll have had the fun of imagining all sorts of wonderful things during our picnic before we find out that your mysterious box is full of mouldy biscuits instead of gold coins.'

'Don't mention biscuits,' Sierra moaned.

'OK. I'll rig up the flag again while you get the food ready. No point in missing out on another rescue.'

After Tash replaced the flag, they sat on the beach near Sierra's HELP! sign and picnicked on Aunt Dina's cheese and pickle sandwiches.

'I've got tuna sandwiches to share.' Sierra pulled a plastic sandwich box out of her handbag. She popped open the lid and the contents went flying. 'Oh, my godfathers!' she cried. Tuna and triangles of bread lay higgledy–piggledy on the sand. She stared at her ruined lunch in despair. Mojo scampered over to inspect. 'Go on, Mojo,' Sierra said. 'Someone should get to enjoy what's left of my lunch.' Mojo hungrily scoffed down the sandwiches. 'What else is there?' Sierra eyed Elly's backpack hopefully.

'No, Sierra,' said Tash. 'We need to keep the stuff that won't go off for later. Just in case.'

Sierra watched sadly as Tash put the crisps, chocolate and apples back into Elly's backpack. 'I'm still hungry,' she moaned.

'You may be even hungrier later.' Tash was at her most

captain-like, brisk and determined.

Sierra nodded and heaved a sigh. Then her face brightened and she rootled around in her bag, finally pulling out a packet of mints with a flourish. 'Dessert and fresh breath all in one!' she exclaimed in a TV advert voice. 'Am I not the perfect castaway?'

'Absolutely!' Elly dissolved into giggles. She and Tash both took a mint.

'And now…' Tash placed the box from the shipwreck in front of her. Elly and Sierra leaned in close. It was a moulded plastic box about the size of a laptop case. And it was covered in slimy algae. Tash grabbed some dried seaweed and rubbed at the box, scouring away the green slime.

'What is it?' Elly was dying with curiosity.

'If it's a laptop it isn't going to work now,' Sierra said.

'It's a boat box,' Tash said, intent on her task.

'A storm box. Waterproof. You can get them any size. Hang on.' Tash didn't look up. She grabbed more seaweed and scrubbed fiercely. Dark grey plastic showed through the slime. Elly could see an aluminium metal plate on the top of the case. Tash's hand slowed and dropped the seaweed. With her finger, she traced the letters Elly could see carved in the metal.

'E. Builtmore,' Tash breathed, her voice barely above a whisper. 'I knew it! We've solved the mystery of what happened to Edith Builtmore. That's her yacht down there. She almost made it home.'

Chapter 10

Elly and Sierra sat back and watched Tash finish cleaning the last of the slime from the plastic box. Elly felt her breath coming faster. It seemed so unreal. She could hardly believe it was Edith Builtmore's boat in the underwater canyon, lying hidden all those years. They had solved one of the greatest mysteries surrounding Sunday Island and its most famous inhabitant. And what was inside Tash's box? Please, Elly thought, don't let it be mouldy biscuits!

Tash pressed on the two latches. There was a click which made Elly jump, and Tash

slowly flipped the latches open. She glanced up at them, her eyes wide. Then she opened the lid.

Elly stared at the contents of the box. It was full to the brim with hundreds of pages of lined A4 paper. Paper covered with slanting, slightly messy joined-up writing, some of it scratched out and corrected in various coloured inks.

'Wow.' Sierra's voice was awed. 'She wrote by hand. How amazing is that? Imagine, writing a whole book by hand.'

'The paper's dry,' Elly said. 'That box really worked!'

Tash touched the top page of the manuscript. 'It's as if she wanted this to be found. It must be the last thing she ever wrote.'

'So it was a treasure boat after all,' Elly said. 'Edith Builtmore's last

book. That's so amazing.' She shivered with excitement as a thought struck her. 'Maybe they'll make it into a film.'

'They should make a film about us finding it!' Sierra paused dramatically. 'And we can star in it! My dad could write all about our adventures. Well...' she hesitated, 'someone can anyway. I mean, we nearly drowned, crash landed on an island, rescued whales and now we've found a long-lost book by a famous author. What more could Hollywood want?'

'Tash found the book,' Elly corrected.

'*We* found it.' Tash gently closed the lid and snapped the latches shut. 'Now we need to get it, and us, off this island and home.'

'I've been thinking...' Sierra hopped to her feet and started to pace. 'We need to build a fire. Up on the hill. A beacon fire. They'd see that tonight on Sunday Island.'

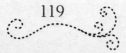

'Good idea,' Tash said. 'But we haven't got any matches. Wait a minute,' her eyes grew bright with excitement. 'What if we try starting a fire the really old-fashioned way? By rubbing sticks together?'

'I've seen it in movies,' Elly said doubtfully. 'But does it really work? I think it's harder than it looks.'

'It's worth a try.' Tash jumped to her feet.

The girls and Mojo climbed to the top of the island. They'd salvaged what they could from the boat. Tash insisted on bringing the plastic case with Edith Builtmore's last book. When they reached the highest point, Tash stared out across the sea. 'I don't understand it,' she began. 'On a normal summer day the sea between here and

Sunday Island would be full of sailing boats and tourist motor launches. I just—' She broke off with a grunt of surprise. 'Elly, where are the binoculars?'

Elly had placed them around her neck for safe keeping. She handed them to Tash. 'What is it?' Elly asked.

Tash peered through the binoculars. Elly stood on tiptoes, shielding her eyes from the sun, which was still high above the horizon, squinting to see what Tash had spotted.

'What is it?' Sierra asked, looking from one friend to the other.

'They're going the wrong way!' Tash shouted. 'Look at them all. It must be every boat on Sunday Island. And they're heading towards the Eastern Isles!'

'It's the whale spotters, isn't it?' Elly asked sadly, as the last sail faded from view. 'They must think the whales are over on the other side of Sunday Island.'

'Oh no,' groaned Sierra.

'Well, it explains why there have been hardly any boats around here today,' Tash said. 'But my mum will expect me back in a couple of hours and knowing her she'll have the whole of the Lifeguard activated. They'll find us. The flag's still flying. It's only a matter of time. But I suggest we get ready for night— just in case. We'll start our fire and rig up the dinghy for sleeping.'

Sierra gave a mournful howl and collapsed in a heap. 'I want a shower. And a proper loo with toilet paper!' she cried. 'I don't want to sleep with mosquitoes!'

'You won't be,' Elly said with a grin. 'You'll be sleeping with us and  Mojo. And we have a bedtime story no one's ever read before.' She patted Edith Builtmore's box.

'We need a fire more

than ever,' Tash said.
'Let's get to work.'

Tash cleared a fire zone. Elly and Sierra gathered a few pieces of driftwood and dry seaweed. Then Tash grabbed some driftwood and a stone and began to pound twigs into fragments. Elly joined in.

Tash positioned the wood in the nest of dry grass, frayed twigs, crumbled heather and seaweed. She started to roll the sticks between her palms. Sierra and Elly crouched close beside her, trying to block the wind.

Elly's eyes focused on the wood, praying that she'd see the slightest ribbon of smoke. But nothing came. After a few minutes, she could tell that Tash was getting tired. A bead of sweat dripped from her friend's brow. Tash's face was beetroot red. At last she sighed and dropped the sticks. 'I guess it *is* harder than it looks. Half this stuff is damp so that doesn't help.'

Without the signal fire, it would take them even longer to get rescued. They could really use the fire when the sun set. *The sun*, Elly thought, *that's it!*

'We could try to use the binocular lenses,' Elly cried, remembering another scene from one of her mother's movies. 'Focus the sun's rays through the lens.'

'Wow,' said Sierra. 'Someone's been paying attention in science class.'

'This could work, Elly,' Tash said, glancing up with a smile. 'Using the binoculars is a clever idea. But we need to hurry before the sun goes down any further, or the rays might not be strong enough.'

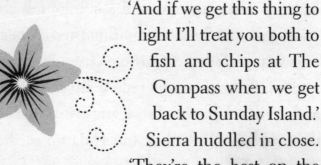

'And if we get this thing to light I'll treat you both to fish and chips at The Compass when we get back to Sunday Island.' Sierra huddled in close. 'They're the best on the

island. I've taste-tested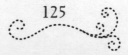
the lot.' She groaned.
'Oh no! I just reminded
my stomach that it's hungry!'
She gave Elly's backpack a longing glance.

'We've only got two apples, a chocolate bar
and a bag of crisps left,' Tash said. 'And we're
saving that for breakfast. If we get the fire lit
I'll find a stick I can sharpen and try to do
some spear fishing down in the canyon. There
were lots of pollack and some small sea bass
there and it shouldn't be too hard to catch
one. If that fails we'll have to try to make a net
with some rope and Sierra's sarong. We can
catch smelts.'

'Leave my sarong out of it!' Sierra cried.

'Do you want fried fish for breakfast or not?'
Tash asked.

'Oh, all right,' Sierra sighed. 'Have the
sarong. But supper would be even better.'
She licked her lips.

'We have to get the fire to light first,' Tash

said. She looked down at their small pile of twigs and wood. 'We're going to need more wood. This might be too damp.'

'I'll go and fetch more driftwood,' Elly said.

'Tash and I can make the bed,' Sierra offered.

'Mojo can help,' Tash added. Mojo wagged his tail encouragingly.

Elly walked back to whale cove. After the battering she'd got in the storm and a day's swimming, her body felt worn out. The sun seemed to be sliding towards the sea quickly now, and the air was definitely cooler. She wondered what it would be like to sleep on Elly Island, under the stars, with the sound of the waves keeping them company all night. It sounded lovely when you thought about it that way, but she knew she might be scared when the time came. Even though

MOJO

they were bound to
be found soon, the
ocean seemed very big,
and this island very small.

She was in a solemn mood as
she climbed down the headland of granite
boulders into whale cove. A few wading birds
took flight as she approached the beach,
skittering in alarm. Elly stood for a moment,
looking at their footprints in the sand, and the
drag marks the raft had made. And there was
Sierra's HELP sign, staring up at a sky empty
of anything but sea birds. Elly shivered. It
seemed suddenly very lonely here.

Something, a movement in the corner of
her eye, or a faint noise, made Elly turn her
head and look out to the cove. A smooth,
wet head bobbed in the water. Large dark
eyes watched her. Elly gasped. And then she
breathed out in relief and felt stupid, even if
her knees were still a bit shaky. It was a seal. A
solitary grey seal, swimming in the cove and

watching her. It was probably fishing. Maybe the same seal who had swum with them earlier in the day.

Elly looked into the seal's eyes, mesmerized. It didn't seem at all frightened of her. It bobbed up and down with the waves, silently staring at her, as though it wanted to tell her something. And then she remembered something she had read once in a book of folk tales. A story about seals being the souls of people who had died at sea.

A shiver ran up and down her spine and Elly took a step backwards. Stop being silly, she told herself. But the thought had lodged in her head and she couldn't shift it. Her heart began to thud in her chest. The seal had guided them to the wreck. It was as though it had wanted them to find the boat and the lost manuscript.

Elly was shivering badly now. Why did the animal keep staring at her? If it was a ghost, Elly didn't want to be alone on a deserted beach with it. She began to retreat, backing slowly away from the water, longing to turn and run but not quite daring. Then she remembered the fire. She needed to find dry sticks and wood. Tash and Sierra were depending on her.

Elly stared at the seal and the seal stared back.

Slowly, Elly began to creep along the beach, squatting and fumbling as she collected driftwood. Each time she looked up, hoping the seal would be gone, it was still there, still watching.

The bits of wood were warm, dried out from the sun. Her nervousness began to fade. The seal wasn't hurting her, ghost or not. And even if it was a ghost—maybe Edith Builtmore—surely it would be pleased with

them for finding the lost book. Elly stood up, her arms full of wood.

The seal still bobbed in the water, its eyes sparkling in the setting sun. The last of Elly's fear drained. Tash said Edith Builtmore had been a brave and good woman who cared about the islands and loved the sea. If ghosts did exist, Edith Builtmore would certainly be a friendly ghost. She stood straight, her arms full of driftwood, and smiled at the seal. 'Goodbye!' she called.

The seal slipped back beneath the waves as silently as it had come. Elly watched the place it had disappeared for a moment, then turned and walked back to her friends.

Chapter 11

It was growing chilly by the time Elly got back to the fire pit. The wind was getting up and a few clouds were gathering in the west. If it was this cool now, what would it be like after dark? Sierra's purple and green sarong fluttered bravely from the flagpole. Tash had fastened two guy ropes to the top of the pole and secured them with heavy rocks. At least their flag was still standing. But it would be useless after dark. They had to get that fire started!

Sierra looked up and waved. 'Hey there. What kept you?'

 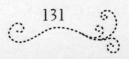

Elly opened her mouth but the words dried on her lips. She couldn't talk about the seal. It was a secret between her and the island.

'Nothing,' she said.

'Everything's ready. We need to light it before the sun gets too low, or your lens trick won't work,' Tash warned. 'Your idea, Elly. You have a go with the binoculars while I break up some of the wood you've brought.'

Elly knelt down, holding the binoculars. It was up to her now. What if she couldn't do it?

'Can you two make a windbreak?' Elly asked. She knelt and twisted the binoculars back and forth, trying to catch a ray of sun and concentrate it on the pile of wood dust and fine fragments of pounded driftwood. She focused a ray of sunshine and waited. Several long minutes later they were still waiting. Elly's hand was beginning to

ache from holding the
binoculars still.

She stared at the
kindling in despair. It
wasn't going to work! Then she caught her
breath. There it was: a tiny curl of smoke. It
got larger, then Elly spotted a red glow. She
blew gently on the glow and with a puff, a
single tiny flame flickered up. Elly fed it the
fragments of wood Tash was handing her.
The fire flickered more strongly.

'Brilliant!' Tash shouted. Mojo, catching
the excitement, began to bark.

'Yippee!' shrieked Sierra. 'Warmth! Rescue!
Fish and chips at The Compass!'

Elly made a tepee of twigs over the flames
and watched with satisfaction as the fire
caught hold and grew strong. Soon it was
thoroughly alight, and Tash was able to put
on larger pieces of driftwood.

The girls each grabbed a cushion and
warmed themselves by the fire. Mojo curled

up by Tash and was soon softly snoring.

'You know what we need now?' Tash said with a cheeky grin.

'Don't say marshmallows,' Sierra groaned. 'You're killing me!'

'Not marshmallows,' Tash said. She walked over to where she'd stored Edith Builtmore's plastic case. 'A story!'

'Perfect,' Elly said. 'We'll be the first people to read the last story Edith Builtmore ever wrote.' Elly thought of the seal and the ship's wreckage hidden for so long under the sea. In some ways reading the story would be like bringing a part of Edith Builtmore back to life.

'I think you should read it, Elly,' Tash said, handing Elly the box. 'You're the actress.'

Elly opened the case. As she picked up the first sheet of paper, her hands began to shake. She studied the page. It wasn't

MOJO

easy to patch the story together. Edith had crossed out sentences and scribbled words with arrows in the margins.

'I'll do my best,' Elly said and started with what she thought must be the title: *'The Mystery of Saturday Island'*.

'Oooo!' Sierra squealed. 'I bet she means Sunday Island. That's what the story is really about. Go on!'

'"Three girls frolicked on the deserted beach,"' Elly read.

'Frolicked!' Sierra interrupted. 'Who says frolicked?'

'Sierra,' Tash said with a laugh. 'At least let her finish one sentence.'

Elly cleared her throat and started again. '"Their laughs easy. Their smiles bright. They were as different as they were alike. One watched the seals and birds, her sketchbook always in her hands. One pranced on the

sand as if performing for an audience and one swam laps in the sea."'

'That sounds like us!' Sierra interjected again. 'Ooops. Sorry.'

'It sounds like our mothers,' Tash said, looking from Sierra to Elly.

'Do you really think so?' Elly said. She could feel the tickle of sadness at the back of her throat. She loved the idea of a story about her mum, a story that everyone could read and know how wonderful she had been.

'Maybe,' Tash said. 'Let's see.'

Elly found her place on the page again and continued, '"They didn't see the dark clouds rolling in. They didn't know their lives would change as quickly as a clap of thunder and dramatically as a flash of lightning."'

'Oh! Oh!' Sierra said and jumped to her feet.

'Sierra!' Tash scolded. 'At this rate we are never going to finish the story or even the first page.'

'But—' Sierra started.

'It's getting good, Sierra,' Elly said. 'Don't you want to know what happens next?'

'Yes, but...I mean...' Sierra was bouncing up and down and pointing.

'What is it?' Tash said. 'What's the matter?'

'Did something bite you?' Elly asked.

'No, but—' Sierra waved her hands wildly.

'What's wrong?' Elly and Tash said in unison.

'I think,' Sierra said, trying to calm down, 'we've been found!'

Chapter 12

Sierra pulled Tash to her feet and whirled her round to face Sunday Island. 'Do you see what I see?'

Mojo started yipping. Elly hurried to close the plastic case containing Edith Builtmore's story. She wanted to read more but she also wanted to go home.

'Look! Look!' Sierra shrieked again, pointing out to sea.

Behind them, the sun floated above the rim of the western ocean. Ahead, the sky was full of a clear, orange-tinged light.

'Sailing boats!' Tash exclaimed. 'Wow!

It's the whole of Sunday Island sailing club out there! And all the tourist launches. And there's the lifeboat!' Tash jumped up and down, shouting at the top of her lungs: 'We're rescued! We're rescued!' She patted Elly on the shoulder. 'They must have seen your fire.'

Elly hardly heard her. There was something in the sea, in front of the boats. At first she couldn't take in what she was seeing. She found the binoculars and lifted them to her eyes. And understood at last.

'No,' she said. 'That's not why the boats have come.' Elly could hardly speak. Her throat was tight and her eyes were stinging. She handed the binoculars to Tash. 'Take a look at the water in front of the lead boat.' She gave a loud sniff and wiped her eyes.

Tash stared at her in amazement. 'What is up with you?

You aren't sad to be rescued, are you?'

Elly couldn't speak any more, so she pointed out to sea. Sierra swooped down on her and enveloped her in a super-Sierra hug before spinning away and dancing around the hilltop.

Tash held the binoculars to her eyes for a very long time without speaking. 'I don't believe it,' she said at last, lowering them.

'You can see them,' Elly said quietly. 'They're leading the boats to us.'

'What are you talking about?' Sierra darted up and grabbed the binoculars. She stared through them for a few seconds, then turned to Tash and Elly, her expression stunned into sudden seriousness. 'That's amazing. Actually, that makes me feel…' Her voice trailed away, and she lifted the binoculars for another look.

Elly could see the whales clearly now. It was almost as though they wanted to be seen.

They swam together, mother and calf, huge dark shapes curving up out of the waves every few minutes. A few times she saw them arch their great backs and dive below the waves. Each time her heart leapt into her mouth, in case they didn't reappear. But just as she was about to give up looking, the whales would break through the waves and jump in the air like enormous dolphins. Once, Elly saw the whole of the mother whale clear the water, to the very end of her tail, and hang for a moment in the air, outlined against the dark blue and orange evening sky.

'I'll never forget this.' Tash was struggling not to cry.

Elly and Sierra reached out at the same time to take her hands. They stood, facing the strange procession: two whales leading a flotilla of boats across a twilight sea.

MOJO

'Me neither,' Elly said.

Sierra was quiet for a moment. 'Gosh,' she said at last in an awed voice. 'It's almost like being royalty. Or… being an alien from outer space…or maybe a criminal. All those people are coming for us.'

'Only because of the whales,' Tash said. 'Although I bet it's my mum that called out the lifeboat.'

Elly found she was shivering, but she didn't feel cold. Tash's and Sierra's hands were warm in hers, and Mojo sat quietly in front of Tash, looking up from time to time into his mistress's face as though wondering why she was standing so still and silent. There was only the sound of waves striking land. Even the wind had gone quiet.

People in the boats had spotted them. Now the faint sound of shouts and halloos drifted towards them. Tiny pinpricks of light sparkled in the dusk: camera flashes.

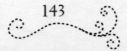

143

Elly and Tash waved.

Sierra clapped her hands to her head, feeling her long, tangled hair. 'Oh my godfathers!' she shrieked in horror. 'I must look a mess. And they have cameras! No!' she wailed. 'I can't have my moment of fame looking like this.'

Tash grinned at Sierra. 'Fame finds you when it finds you.'

Sierra rushed to find her handbag. She pulled out a hairbrush, compact and lip gloss and set about repairing the damage.

Elly watched the whales, mesmerized. Mother and child. Her heart hurt, but in a good way. Tash stood silently beside her. They had the best possible view from up here. Elly couldn't bear to move, lest she lost sight of the whales. They had nearly reached the island now.

She was amazed
afresh at how huge
the mother whale was, and
how beautiful.

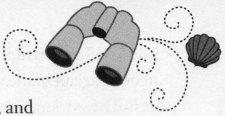

The whales began a slow circuit of the island, keeping well clear of the rocks. Some of the flotilla continued to follow them at a safe distance, the whale spotters on board taking pictures and videos with sophisticated looking cameras. But the lifeboat and two sailing boats headed into the cove where the *Mojo* had run aground. They anchored and Elly could see them getting rubber dinghies ready to launch. But she couldn't tear her eyes away from the whales. Then, almost as soon as the lifeboat entered the *Mojo's* cove, the mother whale dived beneath the waves.

'They're gone,' Elly said sadly.

Tash nodded, but continued to watch the sea.

As Elly was turning away, she heard shouts and cheers from the whale spotting boats. She

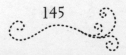

turned back just in time to see the mother and calf cresting out of the water in a huge double jump. There was a splash, a flick of two tails, and the whales disappeared. Elly knew she wouldn't see them again.

'That was goodbye,' Sierra said. Her handbag lay forgotten at her feet.

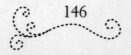

Chapter 13

It was dark by the time the lifeboat chugged into Sunday Island harbour. There was a huge crowd gathered on the quayside. Camera flashes twinkled like Christmas tree lights, and Elly even noticed a TV camera crew. They were going to be on the news! Sierra squealed when she noticed the TV camera. Tash nudged Elly and grinned. Elly smiled back, but she was tired, cold and very nervous. Were they in trouble?

She spotted Aunt Dina in the crowd, looking very dramatic with her long black hair and favourite hand-crocheted shawl flapping in

the wind. Her aunt had a huge smile on her face and Elly felt relief flood over her. If Aunt Dina was angry, you knew at first glance.

One of the lifeboat men threw the rope to someone on the quay and the boat was quickly tied to the moorings. Then he turned to them. 'Out you get, girls. There's some people keen to see you.'

Tash had fastened a piece of rope to Mojo's collar before leaving Elly Island. Now she scooped him up, obviously worried that he would be trodden on in the crush of people on the quayside.

'Do you want me to carry the box?' Elly asked, gesturing to the manuscript case.

'I can manage.' Tash picked up the case with her spare hand.

The lifeboat man smiled at them and held their elbows as they climbed onto the

quay steps. Elly knew
he was being kind,
but she wished he
wouldn't. She wasn't a
frail old lady or a silly little
child. She had made friends with whales,
discovered a sunken treasure boat, braved
a ghost—or at least a very inquisitive seal—
and made a rescue fire. She felt like a hero!
She just hoped her aunt would see it the
same way.

As they clambered up the flight of stone
steps from the mooring onto the quayside, the
night exploded with flashing lights and the
clicking of dozens of cameras. It was just like
being a film star! But right now she was more
interested in finding Aunt Dina, who seemed
to have been swallowed up by the crowd.

'Excuse me!' It was her aunt's megaphone
voice and the crowd parted as if by magic. Aunt
Dina swept up to Elly and pulled her into a
huge, squishy hug. It was a wonderful feeling.

149

'Natasha!' Tash's mum swept through the crowd. She had a huge grin on her face, and for a moment she looked just like her daughter. Mrs Blake-Reynolds grabbed Tash and gave her a hug and a kiss, then stood back and her smile disappeared. 'You didn't tell us where you were sailing. Natasha, this is serious. If I can't trust you—'

'Tell her about the treasure, Tash,' Elly said quickly.

'Don't be cross with Tash, Mrs Blake-Reynolds.' Sierra, arm-in-arm with her father, joined them. 'She's a brilliant sailor. She never lost her cool once when the storm hit us. And she found real treasure on Elly Island! We're going to be *so* famous!'

'Treasure?' Aunt Dina's laugh boomed over the roar of excited voices. 'Gold doubloons, parrots and pirates, eh?

What did you find?'

'This.' Tash held up the boat box. 'We found the wreck of Edith Builtmore's boat and this was on it.'

'You went inside a wreck while diving?' Mrs Blake-Reynolds's voice rang out like an alarm bell. 'That's it! Of all the irrespon —' Her voice trailed off…'Did you say Edith Builtmore? You found the *Builtmore Adventurer*?'

Tash nodded, and her mother shook her head in amazement. 'So the mystery of what happened to Edith is solved at last. You know, she gave me my first sailing lesson.' Tash's mum looked sad for a moment, then nodded at the box. 'Well, don't keep us in suspense. What is this treasure you've found?'

There was an excited buzz in the crowd standing near them, as people caught the name Edith Builtmore. Elly noticed the woman from the TV news ordering the photographer to aim the camera at them.

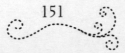

Tash's voice rang out in the sudden hush that fell over Sunday Quay. 'We found Edith Builtmore's last book.' She held up the box. 'It's in here, all of it.'

'An unpublished Edith Builtmore story?' The reporter pushed forward, her microphone already reaching for Tash's reply. The cameraman moved in for close-ups.

Elly saw Sierra finger combing her hair frantically before turning a radiant smile on the camera. She grinned to herself. Sierra was having one of her dreams come true today, as well as Tash. And her? She looked up and found her aunt watching her, eyes full of relief and the fading traces of fear and worry. Aunt Dina gave her a hug. Elly felt the warmth right through her wetsuit.

'Elly! We need you!' Tash and Sierra were posed in front of the TV camera, the reporter  beside them armed with her microphone.

She walked forward slowly, feeling suddenly shy. Tash grabbed her left hand, Sierra the right, and pulled her into a group hug.

'It's been just like one of Edith Builtmore's books,' Tash said.

'Better,' corrected Sierra, whose eyes were glowing with happiness.

Elly pulled her mother's charm out from inside her wetsuit. The silver shone in the glare of the torches and searchlights. Tash patted her badge, safely pinned to the front of her suit. Sierra slid her charm bracelet and bangles out from the safety of her wetsuit sleeve and lifted her arm in a victory salute. Her charm glinted like a shooting star.

'We want an interview, girls,' called the woman reporter. 'Can you look at the camera, please?'

Elly put her arms around Tash's and Sierra's

shoulders. Her heart was thudding with nerves, but even more with happiness. She glanced over at Aunt Dina, and then gave the TV camera a big smile. She was her mother's daughter, after all.

Turn over for a sneaky peek at the next book in The Flip-Flop Club series

Turn over for a cheeky peek
at the next book in
The Flip-Flop Club series

Chapter 1

Elly charged up the hill, her backpack bouncing with each step. The sun was setting and she was late for the sleepover at Tash's tree house.

It was Celeste's fault. Aunt Dina's old friend was staying with them, and she was a little weird. She was obsessed with ghosts. Over supper Aunt Dina had mentioned that Sunday House was supposed to be haunted by the ghost of Tash's grandad, Old Man Blake. Celeste had spent the rest of the meal questioning Elly, even cornering her in the hall as she tried to leave for the sleepover.

It had taken forever to escape.

The Blake family graveyard was just ahead. Elly could see the dark rectangle that was Old Man Blake's grave, which he had ordered be left open and unfilled. Elly skirted past the graveyard and gasped.

A shape loomed out of the gathering dusk. It stumbled towards her, tall, with misshapen shoulders and no head. Elly's heart lurched. It *couldn't* be human—but it had legs. And feet. And . . . flip-flops. Neon pink ones. Another creature appeared, wearing sparkly purple flip-flops. Beside it trotted a small dog.

'Tash! Sierra!'

The border terrier, Mojo, darted up to Elly, barking in delight. Tash and Sierra peered around the cardboard boxes they were carrying. 'Oof!' Sierra dumped

her boxes on the ground. 'Hey, you skiver!' She turned to Elly with a grin. 'You were supposed to help cart this stuff to the tree house. What kept you?'

'Something happen?' Tash put her boxes down more carefully. 'You look worried.'

Elly sighed. 'Aunt Dina has an old friend staying. She's just a bit . . . well. Never mind.' She felt disloyal complaining about her aunt's friend. 'She held me up, that's all.'

'Oh wow! I never thought I'd get to meet an actual survivor of Boring-Grown-up-Guest Syndrome!' Sierra's eyes were wide with awe. 'You're totally my hero. Which means you're forgiven.'

'And you're still in time to help.' Tash picked up one of her boxes and shoved it into Elly's arms.

'What's in this? It weighs a tonne.'

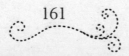

161

'All will be revealed,' Tash intoned in a spooky voice.

'Thanks, guys.' Tash collapsed onto the floor of the tree house.

'Hey, don't damage the slave labour.' Sierra pulled her leg out of the way. She was lying near Tash on her back, groaning at the ceiling. 'I may not live. I need another doughnut, quick!' She stuck out a hand. Elly dropped a doughnut in it.

'Sorry I couldn't get here in time to help.' Elly sat cross-legged on her cushion, nibbling a doughnut and trying not to feel even more fed up with Celeste.

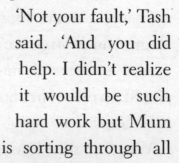

'Not your fault,' Tash said. 'And you did help. I didn't realize it would be such hard work but Mum is sorting through all

Grandad's inventions.
Some of the big
ones are going to a
museum, but she said
I could keep some of my
favourites. I wanted to get
them out of the house now so they don't get
mixed up with the others by mistake.'

They had pulled the boxes up to the tree
house one at a time, in Mojo's dog basket lift.
Tash had only just finished unpacking, and
now the inside of the tree house was piled
with empty boxes and crowded with strange
machines made of wood, plastic, wire,
and glass.

'You'll get my bill in the morning,' Sierra
muttered around the last of her doughnut.
'Trust Old Man Blake's inventions to weigh
a tonne. After all, a considerate person
wouldn't make an open-grave-tourist-trap…
Oh!' She bolted upright, her eyes wide with
horror. 'I'm sorry, Tash! I keep forgetting he

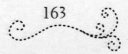

was your grandfather. I mean, he seems more like a story from a long time ago.'

'He died when I was five.' Tash sat up. She wrapped her arms around her knees and rested her head on them, her spiky blonde hair even messier than usual.

Elly thought she looked suddenly very sad. 'Do you remember him?' she asked.

'Yes.' Tash's voice was wistful. 'I know I joke about him like everyone else, but I miss him a lot. He's almost the only thing I do remember from when I was little. I followed him around like a puppy, but he never seemed to mind. Mostly I remember being in his workshop. The rest of the house was dusty and dirty, but the room where he worked sparkled. It was full of shiny bits of metal, tiny coils of wire, boxes of doll-sized screws and

nuts . . . all sorts of tiny, delicate mechanical things. Like a factory run by fairies. And he would sit there at his table, holding these miniature screwdrivers and pliers in his big, wrinkled old hands. While he worked he told me stories about his inventions.' She paused. 'I really loved him.'

'I'm so sorry I said that about him,' Sierra mumbled.

'It's OK.' Tash shrugged. 'I'm used to people thinking Grandad was crazy. Sometimes I think he must have been too. But it was the happiest time of my life. Until I met you two!' She smiled warmly at them, all traces of sadness gone. 'I'm just glad Mum said I could have these inventions to remember him by. She wants the rest to go to a museum. Some professor is coming this week to look at them. Maybe he can figure out what they do.'

'Did your grandfather tell you stories about these?' Elly gazed at the contents of the boxes with new interest. There was something that looked like an old-fashioned electric kettle and a tall plastic tube that looked like a sort of lava lamp. Most of the inventions were boxes of plastic or wood covered in dials and switches. A few had crazy plastic wires looping over their surface. She spotted an unopened cardboard box. 'Hey, you haven't unpacked that one.'

'That one's special.' Tash jumped to her feet, opened the container and lifted out a large, heavy looking wooden box. She placed it on the table and turned to look at them, her face solemn. 'I need you guys to help me solve a mystery.'

WIN
the chance to dedicate

The
FLiP
FLOP
Club

Midnight Messages
to your best friend!

Do you have the best friend in the world?

Are you both huge fans of The Flip-Flop Club?

Go to

www.the-flip-flop-club.com

to find out how you can show your
best friend how much you care.

Terms and conditions apply. One entry per person.
Last date for entries: September 30th 2012.

A Note from the Author

I grew up in Missouri, as far from the sea as it is possible to be in the United States. The long, hot summer holidays were spent swimming and canoeing on the lakes and rivers. My sisters, cousins and I watched crayfish wriggle along the creekbeds, waded in the streams and had our toes nibbled by swarms of minnows darting through the clear limestone waters. We snorkelled in the lakes and pretended we were diving among coral reefs and rainbow-coloured fish instead of Missouri mud and whiskery catfish. Childhood summers were full of barbecues, homemade ice cream, watermelon and twilight evenings spent catching fireflies in order to let them go and watch them spiral into the air like sparks from a bonfire.

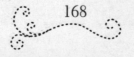

All the time I was growing up, I longed to see the ocean and finally did on a school trip when I was the same age as Elly, Tash and Sierra. I'll never forget swimming with my friends in the sea for the first time.

Now I live in England with my family, and every summer, we spend as much time as we can on an island. My love for British islands is a big part of the joy of writing the Flip-Flop books. On my first trip to the Isles of Scilly I fell in love with the small whiskery dog of one of the boatmen: a proper seadog who trotted around the boat taking us between the islands with a cocky assurance that charmed me. I've been waiting ever since for a chance to write about Mojo! As I write, I'm taken back to some of my favourite places on earth, places very much like Sunday Island.

Ellen Richardson x

Activities
and
Quizzes

Character Profiles

Elly

Full name: Eleanor Porter

Likes: Adventures, stories, films, acting, and hugs

Dislikes: Getting in trouble with Aunt Dina

Favourite colour: Green

Most treasured possession: The necklace that used to belong to my mum

Sierra

Full name: Sierra Cruz

Likes: The two F's—fashion and food! Especially sparkly flip-flops and Aunt Dina's cakes!

Dislikes: Camping, creepy-crawlies, and early mornings

Favourite colour: Hot hot hot pink

Most treasured possession: My friends. And my purple handbag, of course!

Tash

Full name: Natasha Blake-Reynolds
Likes: Sailing, my dog Mojo, being outdoors, seals, sea birds, dolphins, and whales
Dislikes: Letting my friends down
Favourite colour: Purple
Most treasured possession: Mojo—the dog and the boat!

Mojo

Full name: Mojo cute-cuddly-and-cool Blake-Reynolds
Likes: Tash, cuddles, treats, digging, and making new friends
Dislikes: Sitting still

You

Full name: --

Likes: --

Dislikes: --

Favourite colour: ------------------------------------

Most treasured possession: ------------------------

Whale Song Quiz

1. **What is the name of the newspaper that's running the whale-spotting competition?**
   a. The Sunday Island Times
   b. The Sunday Island News
   c. The Sunday Island Gazette

2. **What is the name of the Edith Builtmore book that Elly has in her bag?**
   a. The Secret of Harebell Island
   b. The Secret of Treasure Island
   c. The Mystery of Smugglers Cove

3. **What kind of dog is Mojo?**
   a. A golden retriever
   b. A bulldog
   c. A border terrier

4. **What colour are Sierra's armbands?**
   a. Purple
   b. Orange
   c. Pink

5. **What kind of whales do the girls spot?**
   a. Blue
   b. Minke
   c. Northern bottlenose

6. **Which island do the girls get shipwrecked on?**
   a. Elly Island
   b. Sunday Island
   c. Tash Island

7. **What do the girls use as a flag?**
   a. Tash's jacket
   b. Sierra's sarong
   c. Elly's towel

8. **What does Sierra write on the beach?**
   a. HELLO
   b. SOS
   c. HELP

9. **What does Tash take from the cabin of the shipwrecked yacht?**
   a. A starfish
   b. A plastic box
   c. A pirate treasure chest

10. **What is the name of the fish and chip shop on Sunday Island?**
    a. The Compass
    b. The Tasty Plaice
    c. The Fish Dish

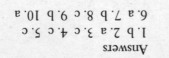

Word Search

The words to the right are all hidden in this grid.
Can you find them?

Z	T	E	L	L	Y	D	S	V	E	F	U
B	M	C	W	J	R	T	H	D	G	L	S
H	A	O	K	Q	O	Y	I	X	Z	I	K
S	N	Z	J	R	B	N	P	D	E	P	W
A	U	T	M	O	G	C	W	R	L	F	E
T	S	R	U	H	V	T	R	B	A	L	R
V	C	J	Y	K	L	A	E	S	H	O	I
H	R	X	T	G	Q	Y	C	J	W	P	F
L	I	F	E	J	A	C	K	E	T	S	P
H	P	R	X	F	M	L	W	K	B	F	M
Y	T	D	O	O	W	T	F	I	R	D	A
C	A	S	T	A	W	A	Y	S	Q	U	C

How to Have a Castaways Sleepover

Unless you're super lucky, you probably can't go on a sailing adventure with your best friends . . . And even if you can, it'd be pretty *unlucky* to end up shipwrecked like Elly, Tash, and Sierra do!

What you can do, though, is have a themed sleepover, where you and your friends are all castaways—stranded on a deserted island . . . (or in your bedroom anyway!) You're unlikely to see any real whales in your bathtub, but at least you won't get any sand in your sleeping bag!

Invitations

Time to get creative! Find pictures of boats, dolphins, whales, campfires, and sunsets to stick on your invites. Or you could make your invitations in the shape of a boat with pictures of you and all your friends aboard!

What to Write on the Sleepover Invitation:
- Date and time of the sleepover
- What to bring e.g. sleeping bag, pillow, trainers, swimming costume, towel . . . anything special that they might need
- Place of the sleepover—You could draw a treasure map on the back of the invitation, marking your house with an X!
- Telephone number for RSVP

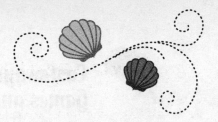

Menu

Castaway food:

- Nuggets of gold (chicken nuggets or scampi!)
- Fish and chips
- Tuna sandwiches
- Coconut ice cream
- Aunt Dina's cakes!—Look at the chocolate orange marble cake recipe in a few pages. This is the cake the girls eat when they're shipwrecked. You can find more recipes in the first Flip-Flop Club book— *Charmed Summer.*

Is your food in waterproof Tupperware? You don't want it getting wet when you go overboard!

Castaway drinks:

- Tropical fruit punch—Look on a few pages for how to make a deliciously fizzy combination!
- Hot chocolate and marshmallows—to warm you up around the campfire!

Castaways Sleepover Games and Activities

- **Where are you shipwrecked?** In your bedroom? In the garden? Better pack your bags with everything you might need! Don't forget a torch and some emergency chocolate! And look out for driftwood — what's washed up under your bed or on the patio that might be useful?

- **What will you wear?** Make fun tie-dye T-shirts or sarongs! Decorate a sunhat! Turn an old pair of jeans into island-ready cut offs! When you've got your outfits sorted, you can have a castaway fashion show!

- **Are there any people living on your island?** Make friends with the natives (your parents and siblings count!) by making friendship bracelets to give to them.

- **Have a treasure hunt!** Give each guest a personalized treasure map that leads to a small treasure, like some chocolate or sweets.

- **Send signals and codes.** Find out about Semaphore flags and learn how to spell your name. Or make up your own secret code and send each other messages.

- **Is the sun going down?** Make stars out of tin foil or yellow/silver paper to stick on your bedroom ceiling.

- **Have a campfire.** But only have a real one if you've got an adult willing to supervise and you're in a garden! Then you can toast marshmallows and stick them between two chocolate biscuits to make "smores"—**Yum!**
- You can also make a great pretend indoor campfire by scrunching up red and yellow tissue paper or material and putting cushions in a circle around it. Very cosy—and no matches required!
- **Play the Campfire Song Maker game.** Think of a popular tune everyone knows (like Happy Birthday), and change the words to be about your shipwreck adventure.
- **Tell campfire stories.** Either share ones you know, or make up new ones together by taking turns to say a sentence—who knows how your story will end!

Whale Song Personality Quiz

What's Your Survival Style?

Imagine that you're shipwrecked on a deserted island…
No one knows where you are, and you don't know
how you're ever going to get back.

How would you feel? What would you do? Answer the
questions below to find out if your survival style is like
Tash's, Elly's, or Sierra's.

1. **Firstly, how would you feel about
   being shipwrecked?**
   a. Energized—there'd be so much to do!
   b. Frightened
   c. Nervous but excited

2. **What one thing would you wish for?**
   a. A boat so you could sail home when you want
   b. A hairbrush
   c. Your best friend

3. **You're bored waiting to be rescued. What game
   would you play with your fellow castaways?**
   a. We'd go on a walk to see who could spot the
   most wildlife!
   b. Truth or Dare
   c. Charades

4. **You've found some driftwood. What will you build?**
   a. A flag pole
   b. A tepee for shelter
   c. A fire

5. **You're hungry. Would you:**
   a. Go spear fishing
   b. Chew your last mint for as long as possible
   c. Keep busy to forget about it

6. **You're going to explore the island. What would you wear?**
   a. Hiking boots
   b. A sparkly sarong—you never know who you might meet!
   c. Camouflage

7. **You write a message to put in a bottle. What does it say?**
   a. "HELP. Shipwrecked. Look for my flag and send a boat!"
   b. "Save me! I need a bath and a real toilet!"
   c. "Sorry I haven't written sooner, I'm just busy having a great time!"

8. **How would you react if you saw a giant spider?**
   a. I wouldn't be surprized—there are all sorts of creepy-crawlies outside
   b. I would freak out completely!
   c. I'd freak out a little, but would try not to scream

9. **What's your favourite thing about sitting round a campfire?**
   a. Getting a chance to relax with my friends
   b. Roasting marshmallows
   c. Telling ghost stories

10. **You've been rescued! How do you feel?**
   a. Relieved. Hopefully I can go back another time and not get shipwrecked!
   b. Thrilled! I can't wait to get home!
   c. Mixed. It was fun, but I'm ready to go home.

Answers

Mostly a's: You're like Tash! – You're a natural leader because you're great at organizing other people to work together as a team. You're also brilliant at staying calm under pressure, which helps those around you to remember what's important. Your practical nature means you're ready for anything, so you're a great person to have around. Your friends are lucky to have you!

Mostly b's: You're like Sierra! – You're impulsive, unique, and a bit mad! Your friends love you because you're so much fun to be around. You're also good at thinking creatively because you don't see things the same way as everyone else. However, when it comes to camping, like Sierra, you're better suited to hotels with bubble bath and no creepy-crawlies!

Mostely c's: You're like Elly! – Your kindness and thoughtfulness make you a great person to have around in tough times, because you always think of others before yourself. You're also naturally optimistic, and brave enough to give anything a try. Team these fab qualities with your lively imagination and your determination and you've got one star castaway!

Cryptic Crossword

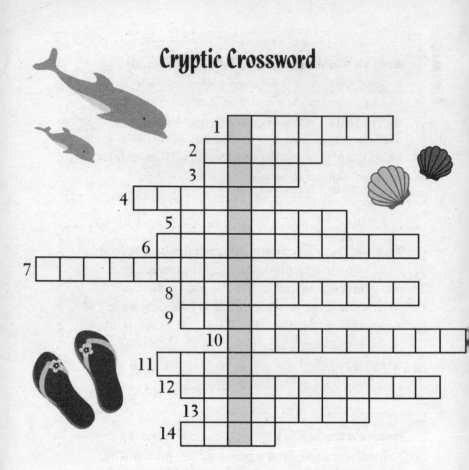

Use the clues opposite to fill in the grid. The number in brackets after the clue tells you how many letters are in the word you're looking for.

When you've finished, the letters in the shaded boxes should spell a phrase. Use this to unlock the secret area on The Flip-Flop Club website!

1. Elly, Tash, and Sierra are this (7)

2. The colour of Sierra's eyes (5)

3. Elly's aunt's name (4)

4. The time of year when Elly, Tash, and Sierra meet (6)

5. Sierra keeps everything in one of these (7)

6. The name of Tash's house on Sunday Island (11)

7. Footwear of choice (9)

8. Even Mojo wears one of these on board the dinghy (10)

9. You read it (4)

10. The surname of the author of The Flip-Flop Club series (10)

11. Elly's aunt is really good at baking this (4)

12. The rocks that shipwreck the girls (11)

13. Tash lends Elly and Sierra one of these each to wear on their sailing adventure (7)

14. Elly makes one of these to keep them warm (4)

Aunt Dina's Chocolate Orange Marble Cake

You will need an adult helper when it comes to using the oven

Ingredients

- 225g butter, softened
- 225g caster sugar
- 3 eggs
- 225g self-raising flour
- 3 tbsp milk
- 1 tsp vanilla extract
- 3 tbsp cocoa powder
- The zest and juice of 1 orange

Method

1. Preheat the oven to 180°C/350°F/gas mark 4.

2. Grease a cake tin and line the bottom with greaseproof paper.

3. Beat the butter and sugar together until light and fluffy.

4. Add the zest and juice of the orange and beat again to combine.

5. Add the eggs one at a time, mixing well.

6. Fold in the flour, milk, and vanilla extract.

7. Divide the mixture into two bowls.

8. Stir the cocoa powder into the mix in one of the bowls.

9. Take two spoons, and use them to dollop the two mixtures into the greased tin, alternating between the plain mix and the chocolate mix. When all the cake mixture is used up, take a skewer and gently swirl it around the tin a few times. This will create a unique marbled effect!

10. Bake for about 45-50 minutes, or until a skewer inserted into the centre comes out clean.

11. Turn out onto a cooling rack and leave to cool.

12. Share with your friends and family – **Yum!**

Tropical Fruit Punch

Mix up this deliciously fruity punch to quench your thirst on a hot day, or to remind you of summer when it's cold outside. It's really easy to make, which is definitely a good thing because it's so tasty you'll want to make it all the time!

Ingredients

- 1 litre pineapple juice
- 1 litre mango or apricot juice
- 50ml lime cordial
- 2 litres lemonade
- Ice cubes
- Fresh fruit for decoration
- Cocktail sticks

Method

1. A few hours before you want to drink your punch, put all the juice and lemonade in the fridge to chill.
2. Once you're ready to start, find a really big bowl and put in a handful or two of ice cubes.
3. Carefully pour the fruit juices into the bowl.
4. Gently pour in the lemonade, being careful it doesn't fizz up!
5. Add the lime cordial and gently stir everything together.
6. Now you can make your punch look really tropical by decorating it with fresh fruit. Oranges, apples, strawberries, kiwi, mango, grapes, and pineapple all work well, so just pick the ones you like! Cut the fruit into bite-size chunks and slices, and put them on a cocktail stick to make your drinks look extra special.
7. Drink up and enjoy!

Try

Different fruit juices like cranberry juice, apple juice, and orange juice can all make delicious-tasting punch. Try mixing up different combinations to make your own unique recipe!

You can also try making ice cubes out of fruit juice. Perfect for adding a quick fruity kick to your glass of lemonade!

Whale Facts

✸ Whales are mammals, like humans.

✸ A group of whales is called a pod.

✸ There are two main types of whale: toothed whales, such as sperm whales; and baleen whales, such as blue whales.

✸ The bones in a whale's fin are similar to the bones in a human's hand.

✸ Whales cannot breathe under water, so have to come up to the surface to breathe through their blowholes.

✸ Most whales can stay under water for about 40 minutes, but sperm whales can spend two hours under the water at one time.

Sperm whales have the largest brain of any creature known to have lived on Earth.

The most dangerous whale is the orca whale, which is also known as the killer whale. Orca whales have 44 sharp teeth and eat fish, penguins, seals, sharks, and other whales.

Orca whales can swim as fast as a car and leap as high as a double-decker bus.

The biggest animal ever known to have lived on earth is the blue whale, which can be up to 30 metres long and weigh upwards of 180 tonnes.

A newborn blue whale is as long as a motor boat and drinks as much milk as fifty human families drink every day!

✳ The blue whale's tongue weighs as much as a baby elephant!

✳ Blue whales are among the loudest animals on the planet. They emit a series of pulses, groans, and moans, and it's thought that, in good conditions, blue whales can hear each other up to 1,000 miles (1,600 kilometres) away.

✳ Humpback whales are famous for their 'songs', which can last for hours.

✳ Narwhals are known for their tusks, which stick out from their foreheads—a bit like a unicorn!

 Northern bottlenose whales, like the ones Tash, Elly, and Sierra spot, are a kind of beaked whale. There are 21 species of beaked whales, all of which are in the toothed whale family.

 Northern bottlenose whales can reach seven tonnes in weight.

 Northern bottlenose whales are one of the deepest diving mammals known, reaching depths of up to 1453 metres.

 Northern bottlenose whales feed mainly on squid and fish.

Read the other books in
The Flip-Flop Club series!

When Elly makes two new friends at a super-secret midnight meeting in a tree house, her summer suddenly gets a whole lot sunnier. Along with Tash's cheeky dog, Mojo, the girls explore Sunday Island – uncovering a mystery that links their pasts, but threatens their friendship . . .

9780192756619

Ghosts don't really exist, do they? Elly, Tash, and Sierra aren't so sure. When their sleepover is interrupted by mysterious lights coming from the graveyard, the girls decide to investigate . . . Is the island haunted, or is there something even scarier going on?

9780192756633

Out May 2013

The stage is set, the lights are down, and the microphones are on . . . It's time for the Sunday Island Music Festival! The headline act is being kept top secret, but they'll be performing on stage with the winners of the Tomorrow's Stars competition, which Elly, Tash and Sierra have entered! If the girls can just get their dance moves in time and their singing in tune, might they be up there on stage with the stars?

9780192756640

Want to join

The FLIP FLOP Club?

Find out more about Elly, Tash, Sierra, and Mojo on The Flip-Flop Club website!

www.the-flip-flop-club.com

Log on for quizzes and activities, as well as exclusive competitions and giveaways!

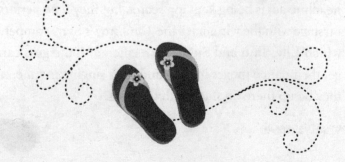